NANCY WARREN

MOSAICS
AND MAGIC

VAMPIRE KNITTING CLUB
BOOK FOURTEEN

Mosaics and Magic, Vampire Knitting Club Book 14, Copyright © 2022 by Nancy Warren

Cover Design by Lou Harper of Cover Affairs

ISBN: ebook 978-1-990210-63-1

ISBN: print 978-1-990210-62-4

Ambleside Publishing

INTRODUCTION

Beware the crystal ball...

When Lucy and Rafe are given a crystal ball as a wedding present, she's shocked when it foretells doom. For the newly-weds, this was supposed to be a time of joy and celebration. But when a terrible accident befalls one of their wedding guests, Lucy and Rafe must postpone their honeymoon. And as the evidence begins to unravel, it becomes clear this was no accident.

Lucy and her undead knitters must navigate punting on the Cherwell River in Oxford, complicated and contentious relationships among their guests, and clues that don't make sense. It may have looked like a random tragedy, but as every knitter knows, when you place the separate strands in a certain light, there's always a distinctive pattern.

~

Get the origin story of Rafe, the gorgeous, sexy vampire in

The Vampire Knitting Club series, for free when you join Nancy's no-spam newsletter at NancyWarrenAuthor.com.

Come join Nancy in her private Facebook group where we talk about books, knitting, pets and life. www.facebook.com/groups/NancyWarrenKnitwits

MOSAICS AND MAGIC

CHAPTER 1

As a girl growing up, I had so many visions of my wedding day. I grew up in the era of Ross and Rachel on *Friends,* and my best friend Jennifer and I used to borrow her mom's romance novels, so maybe I had an unrealistic idea of what love was and what my wedding day to that special someone would be. However, as I looked out at all the people assembled for my wedding ceremony, it suddenly hit me that I was reenacting every fantasy I'd ever dreamed of.

I was about to walk down the aisle in the garden of a beautiful Tudor manor house in the rolling countryside of Oxfordshire. My husband-to-be was wealthy beyond my wildest dreams, beyond any young girl's wildest dreams. He was Mr. Darcy crossed with Heathcliff, with a dash of super-hero thrown in. Unfortunately, the other fictional character he slightly resembled was Dracula. Sure, in my fantasies I'd always imagined a gorgeous, tall, dark, and handsome groom looking at me with the love and adoration that I could see in Rafe's eyes right now, but I'd never imagined I'd be marrying someone undead.

Still, you can't have everything.

He would live the better part of forever, while I was a mortal woman. Well, witch. However, buried deep in one of Rafe's most secure safes was a little box from an alchemist, and inside that box was the elixir of life. A little of that and I could halt the clock on my own aging process. Like Botox for your DNA.

I hadn't been tempted yet, but I hadn't destroyed the elixir either. I liked the possibility that in the future I could always change my mind. It was pretty easy at thirty years old to think I'd never succumb to the lure of eternal youth. I wondered if I might feel quite different as the next decade passed me by. But that was a worry for another day. Right now, I just had to worry about walking down that aisle without tripping.

Beside Rafe was Lochlan Balfour, his best man and fellow vampire, who was as blond and gorgeous as Rafe was dark and handsome. My three attendants all looked back at me, and I felt the support and sisterhood: my cousin Violet, my newly pregnant friend Alice, and my best friend since forever, Jennifer. It was Jen I focused on, knowing if anyone could get me up the aisle in one piece, it would be her. She and I had shared those girlish dreams and fantasies and a few of the raunchier romance novels that her mother never knew about. Or at least we assumed she didn't. Jen was a witch too, something we hadn't realized about each other until recently. I'd been a late bloomer. I was still struggling to understand and begin to control my powers. And, speaking of powers, Margaret Twigg, one of the most powerful witches I knew and the head of our coven, was officiating at today's ceremony. She looked magnificent in her blue robe sparkling with crystal beads. Her gray corkscrew hair was untamed, and her intense blue eyes seemed to laugh at me.

She didn't look as magnificent as I did, though. I was wearing a gown hand-knit and crocheted with the most gossamer-thin of silk. It would have taken human hands years probably to craft this amazing garment, but my vampire friends, all working together, had created and stitched it in weeks. It felt amazing on my skin, not just because of the silk, but there was something magical about the fact that all these creatures who cared about me had taken the time, stitch by tiny stitch, to create something so beautiful just for me.

My mother was standing at the front. She was holding a lace hanky to her eyes, wearing a gorgeous fuchsia-colored dress that flattered her lean figure. I'd talked her into Manolo Blahnik sandals to match, and I had to say she looked fabulous. My mom usually wore jeans or desert fatigues, as she was a renowned archaeologist who spent most of her time in Egypt, so it was a treat to see her look so pretty. She'd even had her hair and makeup done. My dad, also an archaeologist, usually worked with her. So to see the pair of them so dressed up for this special day added a little extra joy.

I took my first step forward, hanging onto Dad's arm. If I looked around at the guests all standing here to help us share this happy occasion, I wouldn't think so much about my feet and whether one was going to trip the other one.

My mom, only having the one child, had understandably wanted to make a pretty big deal about this day. In spite of my arguments, she'd invited more relatives than I knew I possessed. We hadn't seen much of the English ones over the years because I'd grown up in the States and spent summers mainly in archaeological digs or here in Oxford with my grandmother. But she insisted that uncles and aunts needed to be invited, and it wasn't like there wasn't room. Crosyer Manor had acres and acres of grounds. It was just slightly tricky that some of the guests were undead, and it was very important to all of us that that fact not come out today.

My grandmother, for obvious reasons, couldn't be present at the ceremony, and that made me sad. But she had been the one to help me dress, and we'd shared a few special moments. Right now she was in one of the upper windows watching. Before I disappeared underneath the awning, I made sure to look up. The honey-colored stone of the manor house glowed and the rows of windows sparkled in the sun thanks to a recent cleaning. There were three rows of symmetrical windows and my gaze went to the third floor where a couple of the floor to ceiling windows were open. No doubt Gran had opened them, hoping to hear the ceremony with her super vampire hearing. I could picture her running from room to room to catch every view possible. I could just see her face blurred high above me, and I gave a tiny nod. She raised her hand. And then I had to turn my head forward again.

I walked slowly, to the tune of Pachelbel's Canon in D Major played by a string quartet located in the garden.

I was floating in time to the music, holding on to Dad's arm, smiling like a fool because I couldn't help myself, when I became aware that someone was taking my photograph. Oh no. We'd been very clear. There were to be no photographs at the wedding. How on earth could you ever explain the fact that many of the guests and the groom would be missing from any photographs? I glared at the person taking the photos and then recognized her. Why was

I not surprised that the one person who would ignore the only rule we had at our wedding would be my cousin Tina? Tina was that person that your mom makes you invite to your wedding when you really don't want her there. My whole life, whenever we'd come to England, we always had to visit my mom's cousins, and there was this kind of expectation that Tina and I would be friends. We were close to the same age, and that was the only thing we had in common. Frankly, she was kind of a mean kid. I never liked her. And now here she was at my wedding taking pictures. I didn't know what to do.

Then I noticed William, Rafe's butler, the manager of his estates and the world's best caterer, who'd slid unobtrusively out of the kitchens to watch the ceremony. He'd noticed what was going on and then he turned and looked at me and gave me a slight wink. He'd take care of it. One way or another, those pictures would be deleted, and she'd probably never even know it. However, it didn't endear me any more to cousin Tina. She was an unfortunate-looking woman, with lank hair and bad skin, and her choice of dress wasn't the most flattering. She'd gone with a red never seen in nature that grabbed your attention and held it. There were more frills on her dress than in our whole wedding party, and her silver high heels, which I could see because she'd stepped right into the aisle to take the photos, were too high for her to balance on. She wore a fascinator with a bright red feather and too many sequins.

Oh, I was tempted to hit her with a spell that would make that feather take flight and her with it. Kind of like Mary Poppins with terrible dress sense. The vampires would appreciate it very much, but the mortals would have been shocked, and besides, this was my wedding. I'd move my focus to the reason I was here.

When I gazed at Rafe, not even the electric red blot on my landscape could intrude.

I ignored her and kept moving. And then the man beside her took her arm and pulled her back into the space where the guests were supposed to stand. I didn't recognize him and assumed he was her plus-one. He was equally flashy, wearing a white dinner jacket and what looked like diamond earrings. He had that kind of chubbiness of muscle that's gone to seed. He was pretty good-looking but in that way that suggested he knew it and he'd probably been trading on those looks for a long time.

I deliberately moved my attention away from these two and gazed over at the sea of faces that seemed genuinely happy for me and Rafe. We had some good friends, both human and vampire.

It seemed like an eternity when I finally reached Rafe's side. But I hadn't tripped, and I'd actually enjoyed my walk up the aisle. Apart from my annoying cousin, and I wouldn't think of her anymore, I'd felt buoyed by the goodwill surrounding me. Then I forgot all about them as I looked up into Rafe's eyes, usually so wintry gray but lit with warmth as he looked down at me.

"You look beautiful," he whispered. And in that moment I felt beautiful. Then he said, "I thought this day would never come."

But it had. There had been nothing easy or uncomplicated about our courtship, that's for sure. But love can surprise you. It had sure sneaked up on me.

Even Margaret Twigg looked less sourpuss than usual.

We'd considered a Wiccan ceremony but gone with something more traditional, though Margaret would imbue the ceremony with as much magic as she could. It was a great compromise between what my parents wanted and what I'd have preferred. Rafe had also hired a licensed registrar to perform a legal civil ceremony after this one. Margaret was understandably annoyed that her efforts weren't recognized legally, but I'd mollified her by reminding her that, to me, it was her binding us together that would make me feel married.

It might be corny, but I wanted to hear, "Will you take this woman to be your lawfully wedded wife?" and so on. Margaret's voice was strong and commanding, and when we got to the part where I had to repeat, "With this ring, I thee wed," I felt a shiver go over my whole body.

I think until Rafe slipped the wedding ring on my finger and I slipped one onto his, I hadn't really believed that we'd carry it off. I was certain something would happen. I'd had dreams to that effect, where as we were about to say I do, someone yelled, "You can't marry him. He's a vampire." Or a voice would scream, "She's a witch! Burn her! Burn her…" But no. Humans and vampires alike seemed to be perfectly happy for us to join together. And so was I.

The words rolled over me until Margaret Twigg, with a twinkle in here eye, said, "You may kiss the bride."

And then Rafe's lips met mine, cool and confident, the first kiss from my husband. Happiness is never guaranteed and when it comes you have to embrace it. There would be problems between Rafe and me, we both knew that, but for now, in this moment, I'd never been so happy.

We turned and walked back down the aisle together with clapping and congratulations and plenty of tears.

Meri, a 2000-year-old Egyptian witch, and Pete, the Aussie archaeologist, were there. Meri smiled at me through tears of happiness, and Pete sent me a thumbs-up as we passed. Polly and Scarlett, students at Cardinal College and casual helpers in my shop, both beamed as I went by.

My dad's old friend from school, Dr. Simon Pattengale, and his wife, Prunella, nodded. I hadn't seen them in a while, and I had to admit it was nice to see all these faces from the past here to wish us well.

William and I had had long and intense discussions about how we would work out the reception. For one thing, you can never count on the weather here. It was just as likely to rain as not, but our union had been blessed with a beautiful, sunny day. Well, blessed if you happened to be human, not quite so thrilling if you and the sun don't have a great relationship. But William, who'd been doing this a long time, and his sister, Olivia, had planned it so that there were tables inside and tables outside and loads of food and drinks. Lots of tents meant lots of shade. We'd deliberately decided not to have anything sit-down or formal because vampires don't eat the same way we do. But it was very easy for them to put a few bits of food on a plate and wander around. Who'd notice what they ate or didn't?

Lochlan Balfour was Rafe's best man, and after about an hour of walking around and sharing congratulations, he called everybody together onto the stone terrace.

Tina ran to get her handbag and then suddenly shrieked, "Where's my phone?" She glanced around, hand on hip, and glared out at the crowd. "Who took my phone?"

There was an immediate hush as people looked at her askance. Not one other single person had broken our rule and tried to take a photograph. Only her. I'd made a big deal about explaining that we didn't want the distractions. Theodore, a very artistic vamp, was creating paintings of the day, which was charming and so much better than clicks and flashes all day long.

Except for Tina, who obviously thought rules were for other people.

As the bride, I didn't think it would be appropriate for me to tell her in no uncertain terms that her behavior was not appropriate. My mother had insisted we invite her, and when I glared at Mom, she looked suitably horrified but only shrugged helplessly. No help there then. I had a pretty good feeling I knew exactly where that phone was. The waiter, under William's direction, had removed it from her bag. No doubt she'd get it back and her photos would be gone.

It was her plus-one who said furiously, "Stop making that racket. You know you're not supposed to take pictures. Leave it."

"Leave it?" she said shrilly. "That's what you say to a dog when you want it to stop humping your leg."

I realized, in that moment, that my cousin Tina had been partaking rather freely of the free bar. Her date got kind of ruddy around the cheeks and shrugged and walked away. Lochlan, who'd been around longer than any of us, including Rafe, eased away and began chatting to my cousin Violet. He'd let the atmosphere settle before making his speech.

My father, oblivious to the tension, walked up with a tiny cup in his hands. "Lucy, they're serving Boston clam chowder. Look!" As though I might not know what was being served at my wedding. I was thrilled he was so pleased. We'd tried to bring in some tastes of home, like the chowder and tiny lobster rolls, as well as traditional British fare, such as succulent slices of roast beef on miniature Yorkshire puddings, and Scottish smoked salmon. There was caviar on blinis and gorgeous tea sandwiches, and, of course, the vintage champagne from Rafe's cellars flowed. I was sipping the gorgeous wine slowly. I didn't want to end up like Tina.

"And you remember Dr. Pattengale?" There was a twinkle in Dad's eye. Simon Pattengale had taken a medical degree but then transferred to archaeology. His specialty was figuring out what people had died of. My parents were both PhDs but never referred to themselves as Dr. outside of professional associations. Still, Dad and Simon Pattengale had been friends from university days, and they'd stayed close. No trip to the UK was complete without a visit, so I'd known the man my whole life.

"You made a beautiful bride," Dr. Pattengale said. He clapped my dad on the shoulder. "Jack's as proud as punch."

"Thanks."

"Now, Simon, let's get you some of this clam chowder. It's as good as anything you'll find in Boston," and he led his friend away.

Jennifer was standing with my mother, and I went up to the pair of them. My mom beamed at both of us.

"It's so lovely to see you two still such good friends. You were always inseparable as children." And then she turned to my old friend. "And Jennifer, my dear, you look so beautiful."

I agreed, but Jennifer laughed off the compliment. "It's the dress. I'm the girl-next-door type."

A new voice intruded on our conversation. Male and English. "Yeah, you look like the girl next door, if the girl next door was a hot bird."

The three of us turned as one to find Tina's plus-one looking Jennifer up and down with undisguised interest. Then he grinned at her, a grin that he probably thought was terribly charming but looked like a cheap come-on to me. He stuck out his hand.

"I'm Connor Townes. But everyone calls me Con."

Jennifer shook his hand. "Hi. I'm Jennifer."

I asked, "Didn't you come with my cousin Tina Borman?" as innocent as could be.

He glanced over at Tina, who was still rummaging through her handbag as though her phone might magically appear in there. "Nah. I'm just her plus-one. I felt sorry for her, didn't I? And besides, I was keen to see this posh house. Not like he runs tours of the place, does he?"

I thought the main reason Rafe never let strangers into his home was that he didn't want people like this perusing the antiques and artworks he'd been collecting for hundreds of years. Then he leaned in and said something softly to Jennifer that made her laugh. She was clearly able to take care of herself, so I turned to my mother.

Before I could say anything, she said, "I'm sorry I made you invite Tina. She's not behaving very well, is she?"

That was an understatement. "Well, since you made me invite her, I'm putting you in charge of keeping an eye on her. Her date doesn't seem to be doing a great job." We both glanced to where Con was doing his best to impress my bridesmaid. I knew her well enough to see that his cheap charm was not working, but he clearly hadn't caught on yet. I overheard him say something about bridesmaids always getting lucky at weddings. I could have told him that his luck wasn't going to be in, but I'd let him find that out for himself.

CHAPTER 2

*M*om said, "It's a bit awkward because, well, it was Tina who helped us organize the punting."

"What?" That had been my dad's idea, the punting. He'd always loved it when he was a student at Oxford, and as we had so many guests from out of town and a few from out of country, he'd decided to host a punting party the day after the wedding. He thought it would be the most quintessentially Oxford thing for people to be pushed down the river in flat-bottomed boats as a final send-off before the wedding festivities ended. I hadn't particularly wanted to go punting, and Rafe certainly hadn't, but it was so hard not to give in. They hadn't been asked to pay for the wedding of their only daughter, they explained. This was something they wanted to do and pay for, and the event was mostly for their friends and family. Hard to say no.

Now it turned out that Tina had something to do with it?

Mom looked rather sheepish. "In fact, it's her friend there,

Connor, who has a good friend who's got a punting company in Oxford. He got us a good deal."

My heart sank. Connor looked like the kind of guy whose good deals generally turned out to come with a catch. Like that cheap car he gets you that falls apart after you've driven five miles.

I felt slightly sick. "Is it with a reliable company?"

She looked offended. "Your father went to visit them and pay the deposit. He said they're a new outfit, looking to break in. A young man's great-aunt owns this wonderful old Victorian house near the river. That's where they run the business from. I think the house reminded your father of his digs when he was a young graduate. The boats looked perfectly fine, and, as he said, they're flat-bottomed boats floating on a shallow, slow-moving river. What could possibly go wrong?"

I couldn't begin to count the ways. "What's Connor's involvement?" I asked.

"Connor simply said it was one of those things where a friend owed him a favor and he was happy to pull it in for us. Mates' rates, I think he called it."

I didn't want to end up owing Connor anything, and I certainly didn't want to be his mate. My parents would go back to Egypt soon, so they wouldn't find themselves in the position of owing Connor a favor. That would likely fall to me and Rafe. I felt extremely uncomfortable about this turn of events. But it was also my wedding day, and I would put off any unpleasantness as long as I could.

Instead, I turned to find my groom. As though he'd felt my gaze searching for him, he turned from Lochlan and came towards me and took my hand.

"How are you holding up?"

I didn't want to let him know that I was feeling uncomfortable about this deal my parents had made. I wanted him to like my parents as much as I wanted them to like him. We were all family now. I told myself it would be fine and I was overreacting. So Connor got a few pounds off a punting trip. He probably just wanted to act like a big shot. I'd make sure to gush as I thanked him, and I was certain my parents would do the same. Hopefully that would be it.

Rafe said softly, "I think some of our friends will want to leave soon. Lochlan will give his speech, your father wants to say a few words, and I'll wrap things up. Once the formalities are done, then people are free to leave. What do you think?"

"I think that's a stunning idea. We'll cut the cake after my dad's speech, and that's pretty much the signal."

Florence and Mary Watt had made the cake specially for my wedding. They were a pair of octogenarian sisters who owned Elderflower Tea Shop next door to Cardinal Woolsey's. They were happily munching sandwiches they hadn't had to make and chatting happily to the other guests. Their cake was a work of art. They'd used traditional English fruitcake in three tiers and then decorated the whole cake in marzipan, then royal icing. They'd embellished the cake with fondant roses and added whimsy by including marzipan books, a reference to Rafe's profession, and tiny baskets complete with balls of wool, for mine. There was even a cake topper of a couple that looked a little like me and Rafe. I loved it.

I turned to find Margaret Twigg at my elbow, carrying her large bag. Hopefully that meant she was leaving early. Rafe gave her his charming smile and thanked her for performing the ceremony so beautifully. So then I felt like I had to compliment her too. She took our praise as though it were her due and then took me aside and asked me to follow her.

I sent Rafe a helpless glance, but he didn't rescue me from Margaret. Later, we were going to have a serious talk about husband duties, which definitely included saving me from unexpected time alone with Margaret Twigg. "We'll do the speeches when you get back," was all he said.

I felt like crying out, what if I never return?

Margaret began walking, and I followed her. William and his staff had been very careful to make it clear which parts of the estate were open for the wedding and which were off bounds. Polite signs and rope barriers, like at fancy night-clubs, reminded guests where the bathrooms were and made it clear they weren't to trespass. There was still a huge part of the house that was open, so it wasn't like anyone needed to go into the part of the house where the bedrooms were and where Rafe kept his office and his private art collection.

As though she owned the place, Margaret led me into one of the quieter rooms in the older part of the manor house. There were no signs telling us not to come into this wing, probably because William had never imagined anyone would want to. The room hadn't been renovated in at least a hundred years and didn't have much in it, mostly broken things that needed fixing. No one was there.

She said, "I wanted to give you your wedding present."

"That's nice of you," I said. "Shouldn't Rafe be here to open it with me?"

When she shook her head, her gray corkscrew curls bobbed. "This one's only for you."

From her purse she carefully removed a largish bag in black velvet with silver moons and stars embroidered all over it. Somehow, I didn't think it contained a coffee maker or a toaster.

I raised my eyebrows, but I didn't say anything, merely accepted the gift. I opened the silk drawstring ribbon, and as I peeked inside, I could see the spherical ball. I pulled it out slowly, careful not to drop it. I have to say, the crystal ball felt quite natural in my hand. I'd always thought we witches were supposed to choose our own tools, but something about the way it felt suggested I might have chosen this for myself. Had I wanted a crystal ball.

Before I said anything, Margaret Twigg said, "Just because you're married, you can't stop working on your magic. You're a powerful witch, Lucy. You must continue to hone your craft."

I understood what she was saying, but give a girl a break. Couldn't I at least have a two-week honeymoon?

Instead of saying what I was thinking, being the polite witch I am, I said, "Thank you very much. It's beautiful." Exactly what I would have said if she'd given me a set of steak knives or wineglasses.

Her expression soured. "It's not meant to be beautiful. It's meant to be practical. Do you know anything about how to use a witch's globe?"

I'd always thought of it as a crystal ball, but I supposed a witch's globe was just as true. I shook my head. "I've seen Violet use hers. She's very proficient."

"You must do your best to become proficient too. Not every tool becomes our favorite, but each has its purpose. Like your athame, or your cauldron, or your wand."

Light sparked off the surface as I held the ball up. "I've

never used one of these before. I wouldn't know where to begin."

She let out an impatient huff, something that happened frequently when we were together. "You will begin by preparing your ball. Set it outside in the moonlight. For three nights in a row, you must place it under the moonlight, and approaching full moon is best. Be absolutely certain to cover it during the day so the sun doesn't get to it. That's what the bag is for. Plus, that should keep any negative or irrelevant energy away from your ball. I, personally, don't let anyone else touch mine. However, if you choose to do so, make sure you cleanse it of the other person's energy after every use."

I nodded. Leave the crystal ball outside in the moonlight every night for three nights; don't let the sun get to it. I thought I could manage all of that. And if I didn't, at least she wouldn't be around to see it. Although Margaret Twigg had a funny way of knowing everything I did. It was kind of creepy.

Nyx came into the room, then, to see what was going on. I was so happy to see my familiar. She at least was always on my side. Nyx had made sure to steer clear of the wedding festivities, and I'd assumed she was asleep on a bed some-where, but I should have known better. She was keeping an eye on things. My familiar, like most cats, was quite curious. She paced around the room, giving Margaret Twigg a wide berth (she didn't like the older witch any more than I did). Then she jumped up on a stone fountain in need of repair and, like me, she peered into the globe.

Margaret said, "Have you been using your scrying mirror?"

"Sometimes, yes."

"There's a similar technique with a witch's ball. After it's been fully charged by the moon, begin practicing with it. Just you and the ball. Look into its center, and let your gaze be relaxed." For some reason, I did this now even though apparently my ball wasn't yet charged. As though it were a cell phone. Still, I might not like Margaret Twigg particularly, but she was a better witch than I was, and her instructions tended to be useful and to the point. I gazed inside it and tried to look without looking, if that makes sense. I could make out Nyx's eyes glittering on the other side of the ball.

"Settle the mind," she said softly. It was a little hard to do on my wedding day. My attention was not exactly on scrying mirrors and crystal balls. I wanted to be at my own party. Still, if I knew one thing about Margaret Twigg, it was that the quickest way to get rid of her was to do what she asked.

I nodded. "I'm letting my mind settle and looking into the ball but still trying to relax my focus."

"Good. Images and shapes will come up. Let them. Don't try to understand what they mean right away. Just be present and focused."

"Can I ask the ball questions?" I asked.

Another one of those annoyed huffs. "It's not a funfair game where you put in a coin and ask for your fortune," she said.

I moved my gaze from my new ball to her face. And waited. Finally, she said, "You may focus on a question in your mind. Answers may come, and they may not. And when you become adept enough to give a reading, if that's something you choose to do, you will focus on the energy of the other person in the room. Let the ball do the rest of the work."

I looked back into the ball, feeling Nyx on the other side,

her green-gold eyes staring into the ball, and tried to do as Margaret had suggested, but the hardest part was ignoring the presence of Margaret Twigg right behind me like a testy schoolmistress. However, I took a deep breath and practiced looking into the ball. It was beautiful, and it felt really good in my hand. As slightly annoyed as I was that Margaret Twigg was using my wedding as an excuse to push me further in my craft, she had chosen well. Instinctively, I knew this was meant to be my ball.

As I looked, I lost track of what I was doing. I felt a little bit like I was floating and inside that sphere was like a separate world. A dreamlike world. And then when I gazed, I could see the upstairs part of Rafe's manor house. There were people there. I couldn't see their faces, but it felt as though the party were going on without me. Perhaps the ball was reminding me how badly I was neglecting my guests. I was about to say so when something horrible happened. I heard a scream, and then the ball went black.

Nyx made a startled noise, and her back arched.

I turned to Margaret. "Did you see that?"

She looked quite concerned. "I did."

I said, "I don't understand. We haven't even charged it yet."

She said, "It was picking up your energy."

"What does it mean when your ball goes black?" I asked her, feeling panic rise in my chest.

"I don't know, but I suggest we get upstairs. Something's happened." Then she thought for a minute. "Or it's going to happen."

"Can we stop it?" We didn't even know what *it* was.

"I don't know." I started to run out of the room when she said sharply, "Lucy. Return your ball to its bag."

"Right." I had a sense of urgency in my chest, but still I replaced the ball carefully in its bag. If it was this powerful, if it was telling the truth, it was going to be a useful tool.

I set down the now-covered ball on a table with a broken corner, and together we hurried back to the reception.

What would we find when we got there? Who had screamed? And why?

WHEN WE GOT BACK to the wedding reception, everything looked perfectly normal. No one was screaming or injured. The canopy hadn't fallen on the guests or any one of the nightmare scenarios that had flashed through my mind as we raced back here.

I wondered whether Margaret had given me a joke crystal ball. But I no sooner had the thought than I dismissed it. Margaret Twigg was not the joking type.

Trying to shake off the unsettling experience, I plunged into the festivities. Scarlett and Polly were joking with Violet and Liam, a guy who'd been in a college production of *A Midsummer Night's Dream* where I'd helped Theodore with the scenery. I was pretty sure Violet had a soft spot for him and was disappointed to see he had a woman with him. She was a very pretty woman, with thick dark hair and full features, wearing a stunning green dress. Polly introduced her as Georgia Montefiore. "She goes to Cardinal College too," Polly said.

Georgia smiled, showing even white teeth. "Congratulations on your wedding," she said in a posh voice.

I thought that Liam was punching above his weight already having such a stunning date, and yet he seemed oblivious to her. He was making Violet laugh about something, and she was flirting up a storm.

I'd always noticed the warmth between Violet and Liam, and in fact, it was Vi who'd asked me to invite him. If he preferred to spend time with my cousin than his gorgeous date, then perhaps Liam was seeing Violet as more than a friend. I could never tell with Violet. I'd thought she was crushing on William, now she seemed to have rekindled her interest in Liam. Was the student actor a better fit for her than the more mature William? I was pondering the notion of Violet happy in love when a shrill and horrible cry rent the air.

My whole body stiffened for a second, but then I relaxed, realizing the cry wasn't human but peacock. I was accustomed to Henri, a resident peacock who was more pet than wildlife. He was perched on the roof looking down on the festivities. Henri was an overfed mooch, but I was quite fond of him. He liked to eat out of my hand, and Rafe said he had a crush on me, as he tended to fan out his tail when he saw me approaching. His tail had been a bit bedraggled when I first met him, but it had improved a lot. I thought he was letting us know he was present and feeling peckish, though he wouldn't come closer with so many strangers around. Maybe that's what my ball had picked up. An annoyed peacock letting out a screech.

Rafe came over to me and said, "Ready?" I nodded, thinking the sooner this reception ended, the sooner I could relax. I hated feeling that something bad might be about to happen without having a clue what it might be. If this was what crystal balls did, I wasn't sure I was a fan.

Hand in hand, Rafe and I made our way to where Lochlan was obviously ready to go. Once more, Lochlan asked for everyone's attention, and once more we all gathered around. I searched for Tina just to make sure she would keep quiet and was surprised not to see her. That bright red would be visible from space. Still, with so many people gathering round, she was hidden from view. I didn't spot Connor, either. If luck was with me, they'd already left.

And then Rafe put his arm around me, and we both turned to listen to Lochlan, and I forgot to worry about anything else. Lochlan Balfour was a lot older than Rafe. He'd been a Garter Knight. We're talking like 1200. He was the oldest vampire I knew. He was also gorgeous, cultured, and elegant. He lived in Ireland in a remote castle and was a wealthy tech genius.

I didn't think Rafe was any slouch in the wealth department either, but it didn't matter to me. In fact, frankly, I didn't really want to know. He owned Crosyer Manor, and I knew Rafe had other properties around the world as well as priceless art and who knew what investments. Money was never going to be an issue. He could have acted like one of the idle rich, but he didn't. He enjoyed his business evaluating and restoring old manuscripts. I didn't plan to be idle either. I might be marrying rich, but I loved running Cardinal Woolsey's Knitting Shop. I had no intention of giving it up, though I imagined I wouldn't be in the shop quite as much as I had been previously. I wanted to be able to travel with Rafe and frequently see my grandmother, who was planning to move to Cornwall.

Lochlan began by saying, "I've known Rafe Crosyer longer than either of us cares to admit." There was a soft chuckle from my groom and polite laughter from people who had no idea how long they had actually known each other. Since Rafe had been a spy for Queen Elizabeth—and I mean the first one—he was at least five hundred years old. They'd probably known each other for a good portion of that. It was mind-boggling to think of the history these two had experienced firsthand.

Lochlan continued, "But Lucy I've only known a few months. And yet, I sensed the first time I saw these two together that they were destined for each other."

A shiver went over me. There was something about that word *destined* that sounded portentous. But he was right. Some strange force of circumstances had pulled Rafe and me into the same orbit. I mean, what were the chances that I, a woman who'd grown up in Boston and didn't even know how to knit, would end up running a knitting shop in Oxford, or that Rafe, a sophisticated five-hundred-year-old vampire, would belong to a late-night knitting circle in that very shop? It was crazy.

He gave a beautiful speech about love and its importance in brightening our lives, and there was barely a dry eye by the time he finished and asked everyone to raise their glasses to Lucy and Rafe. Rafe spoke next, thanking my parents and complimenting each of the bridesmaids. He was also a very practiced public speaker, but his words felt really sincere, and then he looked at me and I knew he hadn't rehearsed this part at all.

He said, "And to Lucy, I want you all to know, and to say this in public, that I didn't know you were the woman I was searching for until I found you." I was so happy, I thought my heart would swell to the point that some of the stitches on this beautiful dress would burst.

My dad came forward then, fishing his glasses out of the pocket of the new suit Mom had made him buy and finding the handwritten pages of a speech. Dr. Jack Swift looked exactly like what he was, a slightly absent-minded professor who was probably more comfortable digging up long-buried bones in the desert than chatting at a wedding reception. But he was doing his best. He looked out at the crowd over the top of his reading glasses and gave his engaging grin.

"I usually am asked to speak on subjects I'm an expert in. Like the empire of Ramses II or diseases among the ancient Sumerians. I have much less expertise about marriage. I've only done it once, you see." Here there was a smatter of laughter and a little bit of applause. My mom dipped her head. They weren't the most conventional couple, my parents, but they really were an example of how to make it work. Dad continued, "I don't know that a father ever thinks there's a man on earth good enough for his daughter. But I have to say, Lucy, your choice comes close." He was so right. I leaned against Rafe, feeling his strength and tenderness, and my dad continued.

He was talking about the few things he'd learned about keeping a marriage going and managing to make us all laugh when suddenly a woman screamed and pointed.

Oh, no. It was the scream I'd heard when I held the crystal ball. In horror, I followed her pointing finger and was just in time to see a body fall and hit the pavement of the courtyard.

CHAPTER 3

There was a nanosecond of utter stillness as the horror of the moment combined with the social awkwardness of my dad still standing there in the middle of his speech and everyone holding their champagne glasses waiting to toast.

And then the moment broke, and a lot of people ran forward at once to the body lying on the ground. William got there first, followed by Rafe, who had moved at superhuman speed. The two of them prevented me from seeing the upper part of the body, but the fall victim was wearing the uniform of the waiters. I glanced up and saw an open window several floors above him. Even as I felt the shock and horror of the moment, part of me was wondering what on earth one of the waiters had been doing up in the top part of the house. It was where Gran had been watching the wedding from.

People were crowding around, and Lochlan suddenly took charge and said in his commanding tone, "Let's keep back and give them space."

The sun wasn't strong, but I didn't want Rafe and Lochlan

standing in it. Fortunately, William quickly got a couple of the waiters to help him move one of the catering canopies that had been covering a table of food. It was a brilliant move, as it both protected the vampires from sunlight (all the fabrics used were UPF 50) and helped screen the victim from view.

We all obeyed, stepping back about ten feet, but no one was going to go back to their cocktail party now. We all stood there basically staring at this horrific scene. Then a man came running forward. It was Simon Pattengale. "I'm a doctor," he called, sounding out of breath. "Let me through."

Rafe looked up and caught my eye and shook his head. But it was too late. There was nothing I could do to stop him. Dr. Simon Pattengale joined William and Rafe beside the body. He put his fingers to the wrist. I heard him say, "There's a pulse, but it's very slow. And his body seems to be cooling."

And then I realized why Rafe had given me the head shake. The guy on the ground was no mortal waiter. He must be a vampire. And then a few seconds later the doctor said, sounding amazed, "He's conscious."

There was a huge collective sigh of relief and some spontaneous applause.

In a loud voice, William said, "He's only stunned. We'll take him to hospital and have him checked out."

Rafe got up and moved away, and between him and Lochlan and my dad, managed to get everybody back on the veranda or in the house. Dr. Pattengale continued to fuss, and I heard the guy on the ground say, "Really, sir. I'm fine. Nothing broken."

Some mumbling, then, "No. I didn't lose consciousness. Just had the breath knocked out of me."

I had to get Dad to haul his well-meaning friend away from wanting to examine the guy who'd fallen. William helped the vampire to his feet, and we all watched as he rather theatrically limped toward the kitchen and William's quarters.

There may have been some acting 101 involved in the scene, but it did the job. Everyone relaxed and went back to celebrating our wedding.

The story they gave out was that the waiter had gone in to fetch something from the house and accidently fallen out of a second-floor window, but he was unharmed. Taking him to the hospital for observation was merely a precaution.

I knew there was more to the story than that. The second-floor window hadn't been open. But the third-floor one was. It's up where Gran had been watching from. However, I played along. Rafe would tell me what was really going on when he was ready.

At least I hadn't been cursed with a death in the middle of my wedding reception.

The guy who'd fallen out of the window was already technically dead.

MUCH LATER, I could finally relax. The guests had gone. Even my parents had been convinced to leave, mainly because they could escort their friend Dr. Pattengale and his wife, Prunella, home. He was still a little shaken. He kept saying, "I don't understand it. That young man should have been badly injured at least. And yet, his pulse was slow, but he had one. And what a remarkable recovery.

They say he was sitting up before he even got to the hospital."

I knew perfectly well that the vampire waiter hadn't been near a hospital. William had made a show of sending him off with another waiter, presumably also a vampire, but no doubt they'd only gone somewhere to hide until the wedding reception ended.

We all tried to soothe Dr. Pattengale, and my father reminded him that medical miracles happened all the time. He'd just been lucky enough to witness one. William had been wonderful, wandering among the guests, putting out a plausible, if untrue, story that the waiter hadn't fallen out of the top floor as it looked like, but had been fetching a special plate William had needed from the first floor. Even though the woman who had first witnessed the fall kept saying, "But I'm sure I saw him fall from the third story," in light of William's calm explanations, people soon believed him, including the eyewitness. She said as she was leaving, "I'm so glad he didn't fall far. And instead of ruining your wedding, I would think that somebody who survives a fall and walks away to tell about it ought to be a good omen for your marriage." I quite liked that idea and gave her an extra-special hug as she was leaving.

Alfred drove my parents and the Pattengales back to Oxford, and then I went to collect my crystal ball and place it outside in the moonlight. I had a feeling that Margaret Twigg would check to make sure I'd done as she instructed, never mind that it was my wedding night.

The moon was rising, and I went to a quiet part of the garden, an enclosed rose garden that Rafe said had been there when he first built the home. I loved the quiet there and the mixed scents of roses and lavender. A statue of Artemis presided over the walled garden. I knew it was Artemis because Rafe had told me. She was larger than life, leaning against a column, legs crossed at the ankles and a hand on her hip. Her robes draped to her knees, and the rest of her legs were bare. A bow and arrow were by her side. I knew she was goddess of the hunt, but I liked to think she kept the bow and arrow to protect the garden from negative energy. A fountain splashed at her feet, sliding finally into a still pool that glinted with moonlight.

I removed the crystal ball from its black velvet bag and, on instinct, took it to the pool. Moon water was excellent for cleansing magic tools, and I wanted to get any trace of Margaret Twigg cleansed away before I used the ball. No doubt this moon water wasn't the strongest in the world, but it would do for my purposes. I dipped the smooth crystal into the moonlit pool and then placed it on top of a sundial where it could bathe in moonlight unobstructed.

In a soft voice, I said:

> *As you gather strength in the moon's light,*
> *Use that energy to improve my sight.*
> *May my knowledge increase*
> *To help others find ease.*
> *So I will, so mote it be.*

I left the ball watched over by the stone goddess.

When I returned to the manor house, I slumped back in my favorite chair in the lounge overlooking the garden, where the catering staff were clearing up the mess.

Normally we'd have been expected to take off on our

honeymoon. However, so many people had come over from the States and other parts of the world for our wedding that it seemed churlish to run off. I wanted a little time with my folks before they headed back to Egypt and time with Jennifer, so we'd decided to leave on Monday.

The only event left was the punting. None of the vampires had signed up, but as my parents had mainly intended it for family and friends, it didn't matter. They didn't expect me and Rafe to go, which was good.

Still, I felt nervous about the punting expedition. Between discovering that Connor, "call me Con," had wangled a special deal for us and worrying that someone would get hurt —probably my dad, who insisted he still remembered his punting technique after all these years—I'd be glad when it was over. The wedding had gone better than I could have imagined. Even a vampire falling from a great height hadn't been fatal. The last thing I wanted was to jinx it now.

"Don't borrow tomorrow's troubles today," Gran reminded me, happy to be joining us now that all the guests had left. She and Sylvia were busy comparing notes. Gran had seen things from her bird's-eye view that no one else could, while Sylvia could fill her in on the goings-on at the wedding. It wasn't perfect, but at least Gran had been at my wedding in some fashion.

Jen slumped on a couch, still looking gorgeous in her wedding makeup and bridesmaid dress. Lochlan wasn't a slumper. He was still cool and elegant in his formal suit. Rafe had taken off his jacket but otherwise looked equally cool and elegant. I stared at the pair of them. One dark, one fair, both gorgeous, intelligent, and obscenely rich. I turned to Jen, wondering if there was any chance she and Lochlan might like each other, even though I hadn't picked up a hint of interest on either side. I just wanted a reason for her to stay. I was so going to miss my BFF.

Nyx came daintily into the room, gazed around and then walked over to me and jumped up to curl beside me on the couch.

"Careful," Sylvia scolded. "You don't want cat hair on that lovely gown."

"Oh, let be, Sylvia," Gran said. "She'll not be wearing it again."

Sylvia's mouth turned down. "Such a shame, but I suppose you're right. It's like when Coco designed me a perfectly lovely gown for a one-night performance at the Royal Albert Hall. All in black and silver, I was. I wore a Cartier diamond set given to me by the count."

"Which count, dear?" Gran asked. She was always interested in Sylvia's stories of her famous career, and love life, in the 1920s. But the star of stage and screens long past thought for a second and shrugged, "One of them. Or perhaps it was the duke?"

William came in then. Before I could rave about his fabulous food, I realized he had someone following him.

Lochlan turned as though he'd expected this. "Ah, Guy. Good." He turned to address the room. "Allow me to introduce Guy Scovolo." I glanced at Rafe, but he was being inscrutable. Not an uncommon look.

"Perhaps you can tell us how you came to fall out of a window?" Lochlan asked. There was no suggestion of blame. In fact, I suspected Lochlan already knew the answer and wanted the rest of us to know. For some reason, butterflies started dancing in my stomach.

Guy Scovolo was the vampire who had fallen out of the upper-floor window and lived to tell the tale, or not, as you define vampirism. We could finally ask him what had happened.

"I was in the house just, well, it was like William said. I had to go in and get a special plate."

"Oh, come clean, boy," Lochlan said. He turned to Rafe looking slightly sheepish. "Guy is one of my security experts. You know how you are about security. Hopeless. I decided to bring a couple of my people along to keep an eye on things. That double-sided art gallery you've got alone has millions in old masters."

Rafe gave a snort at that. "Not millions, mate. Priceless. I've kept the miniature Queen Bess gave me, you know."

Lochlan gave a low whistle. "Even when she was alive, that was a precious gift indeed. How many miniatures still exist of Queen Elizabeth I?"

"Fewer than half a dozen, I'd wager."

Lochlan was always more interested in commerce than Rafe, I'd noticed. He pursed his lips and thought for a minute. "The miniature alone would be worth untold millions."

"Well, we'll never find out because I'm not selling it. It's priceless to me because she gave it to me with her own hands."

Then he turned to me. "Have I ever shown it to you, Lucy?"

He probably had, but honestly, I didn't remember. He had given me a tour of his personal art gallery, which was cleverly designed so that the walls displayed extremely good and valuable paintings but every panel could be flipped around by turning a discreet brass knob, and on the other side were the real treasures. Even I could identify a Rembrandt. There was a Van Dyck, some sketches by Leonardo da Vinci, lots of impressionists, though he was partial to Van Gogh and Turner, and there was an entire wall devoted to Picasso. Naturally, he'd met the painter and they'd talked about art in Gertrude Stein's house in Paris.

Lochlan looked slightly impatient. "Later." And he looked at us with a funny expression. "If looking at art is how you choose to spend your wedding night."

Rafe threw a shoe at him.

Lochlan dodged out of the way and laughed. "Okay, Guy. What did happen to you?"

Guy relaxed now that he could tell the truth. "I was taking a walk around the house like you told me to. I'd checked out the room with the paintings, and it was undisturbed. I was just about to come back out when I heard a noise from upstairs. It sounded like somebody in trouble, so I dashed up."

"Somebody in trouble?" I asked.

He glanced at me and then away again. "It was your grandmother."

I looked at Gran. "What were you doing?"

"If you must know, I was singing. I felt so sad not to be a part of the ceremony that I sang 'Here Comes the Bride.' This poor young man mistook the sound of my singing for, well..."

"Wailing," he said.

She looked a bit embarrassed. "My voice was never my best feature."

"I didn't know she was up there. I looked into one of the rooms, and the windows were wide open."

"What?" Rafe said.

Now my grandmother looked truly miserable. "It was me, you see. I opened them so I could hear the ceremony. You know how good my hearing is since I've been turned."

Rafe clamped his lips together. I so felt for her. Of course she'd wanted to hear the ceremony where I got married. She wisely didn't say anything, and then Guy continued his tale.

"I suppose I took a moment just to look down on the gathering and make sure there was nothing untoward."

Lochlan nodded. "Good instincts."

He shook his head. "But what happened next showed terrible instincts, and I admit it. I didn't even sense danger. One minute I'm looking out, making sure everything is as it should be, and the next minute somebody shoved me from behind and I was sailing down to hit the ground. I didn't catch so much as a glimpse of my assailant." He glanced at Lochlan. "I'm truly sorry, sir."

But Lochlan didn't seem particularly angry. "These things happen." And then he turned a sharp eye on Rafe. "And now you know why I wanted to get some security in your house."

Rafe looked irritable. I had a feeling this was an old argument between him and Lochlan, the technology and security expert. Rafe said, "Anybody who steals from me is extremely foolish."

Lochlan shook his head. "That might have been true a hundred, two hundred years ago. But the world's moved on, Rafe. Thieves are more sophisticated every day. What if something had been stolen? How do you think you'd get it back?"

"Well, nothing was, was it?"

Lochlan turned to me. "Lucy. Please accept, as my

wedding gift to you both, a full security system for Crosyer Manor."

Oh, I wasn't getting in the middle of this one. I glanced at my new husband. "If Rafe wants to accept it, that's up to him."

Lochlan raised his hands. "You're as bad as he is. And as mad."

Probably.

"Did you have my cousin's phone on you?" I'd seen Guy with my cousin Tina's phone. Unlike the vampire, it probably hadn't survived the fall. I wasn't sure what to tell my cousin when I gave her back a smashed phone. Mind you, it was her own fault for ignoring our one cardinal rule about no photos. I supposed, Rafe being Rafe, that he would buy her a brand new one to replace the one she'd lost. But to my surprise, William pulled the phone, undamaged, out of his pocket.

"Guy had already handed it to me. I was waiting for a convenient moment to give it to Lochlan so he could make those photographs disappear."

Lochlan held out his hand, but I said, "Wait."

I didn't want those photos to disappear before I'd even seen them. Okay, it was egregious of cousin Tina to snap photographs when she'd been expressly told not to. But the ones she'd taken that I had seen were of me and my dad coming down the aisle. Theodore had been busily painting, which was wonderful, and we'd have his beautiful sketches and paintings of our wedding to remember forever. But a few candid snaps of me and my dad? Surely, I could have those.

Rafe seemed to understand and looked over my shoulder as I tried to open her phone. Naturally, it was password-or-fingerprint protected. I made a sound of annoyance, and then once more, Lochlan held out his hand. I honestly had no idea what he did. He took something out of his pocket, and he used his own finger, and next thing the phone was open. I was delighted with him. And much less delighted with Tina. She hadn't just taken photographs of me and my dad, which I'd keep forever, but all sorts of random photographs. She was one of those people who seemed to take photos for something to do. I flipped through and there was one of her and Connor, his meaty arm around her shoulders, a big, golden ring glinting off his finger and his diamond earrings sparkling in his ears.

I flipped through the rest, which were mainly a bunch of crowd shots, and then said, "Wait a minute. Look!" I showed the phone to Rafe, and Lochlan came over and looked over our shoulder. It was definitely Con walking into Crosyer Manor.

I glanced up at Rafe. "Why would Connor go into that part of the house?" It was very clear that was the private area.

He shook his head. "I don't know."

"Looking for the toilet?" Jennifer asked.

"But they're down here and clearly marked." In fact, Rafe had installed bathrooms in a section of the old stables specially for the wedding. They were convenient to the reception and nicer than a five-star hotel. So why would Connor have walked into the main house?

Lochlan looked quite perturbed. "Connor Townes is exactly the sort of person you don't want having a look around your house." He gave the pair of us a hard stare. "I'm putting a rush order on that security system."

To my surprise, Rafe didn't argue with him. He just nodded once.

I got Lochlan to download all the photos Tina had taken

of the wedding from her phone onto my computer, and then I'd decide later which ones I wanted to keep and which ones I wanted to delete. Having done that, Lochlan deleted them all permanently off her phone. It was as though they'd never existed. To make absolutely certain they were gone, he flipped back. The last photo before my wedding was of her and Connor standing in front of an old dark green sports car. "Looks like a Jensen Interceptor," Lochlan said.

He showed Rafe. "Didn't you have one?"

Rafe glanced at the photo. "I had a Jensen Interceptor when it first came out in the 1960s. This is later, '70s maybe."

"He probably got it cheap," I said.

"Or stole it," Lochlan added. He handed me back Tina's phone. "You'll make sure she gets it back?"

The last thing I wanted was a reason to visit my awful cousin. "I guess."

Rafe took my hand and gave it a squeeze. Jennifer had obviously witnessed the gesture, for she suddenly stood.

"Okay, everybody, I think it's time we left." Sometimes I loved her North American directness. As though they'd all suddenly realized at once that they were intruding on our wedding night, everyone rose at once.

"Yes, of course," Lochlan said. "Jennifer, do you need a ride?"

She shook her head. "Theodore is driving us home, thanks." Theodore was waiting for Gran and Sylvia. She could easily have let Lochlan drive her home. My hopeful idea of a match was fizzling by the second.

When everyone left, and even William had wished us goodnight and disappeared to his own quarters, Rafe turned to me.

"Are you sure you didn't mind spending our wedding night here? It's not too late if you want to go to Paris or New York or Bali. We could take off within the hour."

I chuckled softly. Would I ever get used to the unlimited resources of this man? I shook my head. "This is exactly where I want to be. Tonight and forever." And as I said those words, I realized how true they were.

"That makes me very happy," he said. "And now, my beautiful wife, we're finally alone." And then he kissed me.

CHAPTER 4

I was enjoying my first breakfast as a married woman, perfectly prepared by William, who was always happy to have a human to cook for.

Having visited the walled garden this morning to bring in my crystal ball, I'd also gathered some of the roses to put in a vase for our breakfast table.

My eggs Benedict was perfect, and Rafe drank something out of a cooled thermos mug that I didn't inquire about. I thought dreamily of all the mornings like this that stretched ahead of us. I didn't intend to become a lady of leisure. I'd still run Cardinal Woolsey's Knitting Shop, if only to calm down the jumpy vampires who'd been worried I might sell the place. They needed a safe retreat for their late-night knitting club, obviously. But also, I'd learned to love the place on my own. I enjoyed seeing the business grow, and even as I was slowly learning to knit myself, it was fun to teach other people. Well, I didn't do the teaching, obviously, but it was a pleasure to see the number of people who were taking part in our classes.

Rafe was also not one to sit around. I knew he had no intention of giving up the work he loved. As he'd once told me, one of the worst pitfalls to becoming a vampire was boredom. I was thinking about that when I suddenly said, "Rafe?"

"Yes, my darling?"

"Do you think you'll get bored with me?"

First his eyes opened wide in honest surprise, something I didn't see very often, and then he laughed aloud. "I can think of many words to describe how I feel when I'm around you. Bored is not one of them. If you're not surprising me with a question like that one, you're making me see some moving picture—movie," he corrected himself. "Or dragging me in to help solve a murder."

"I do enjoy expanding your cultural knowledge," I said, feeling smug. "But that should end now. Murders, I mean, not movies."

He raised his eyebrows skeptically at that, but I was certain, now that I was living a quieter life as a married woman, the odd and rather unpleasant habit I'd had of stumbling into murder investigations would end. I was very certain the local police force would agree that that was an outcome very much to be wished. Not that I hadn't helped the local CID. I'd even solved a few murders all on my own, but somehow the police never seemed to appreciate my effort or the efforts of my undead helpers. Anyway, I wouldn't think of something as unpleasant as murder on my first day as a wife.

Rafe still had a crease between his eyebrows, and I knew him well enough to say, "What is it?"

"I'm worried about our honeymoon. It doesn't seem, I don't know, grand enough."

I loved him so dearly. Never so much as at that moment. "But it's what I want. Driving down to Cornwall with you and spending time there is exactly what I want. There'll be loads of time for us to jet around the world, but for now, I just want time to get to know you better." I didn't say, but Rafe also had a property down there that I'd never seen. And, if I was going to be completely honest, I wanted to help Gran get settled in her new home. She'd finally decided, with a little bit of gentle persuasion, that it was time for her to move out of Oxford. In Cornwall she could live a much more normal life. She could go out occasionally, and the chances that anyone from our small area of Oxford would recognize her were pretty slim. If Gran was ever unfortunate enough to actually bump into someone she knew, I had to hope there'd be another witch around to perform the forgetting spell. It had worked every time so far, though there had been a few near misses.

"Besides," I said, "I want to see the knitting shop they choose." Rafe's business agent in Cornwall had narrowed the selection of properties that would make a decent knitting store down to three, and Gran and Sylvia would tour all of them. Even though this would be Gran's shop, which she'd staff with a local manager, I wanted to be involved. At the very least, I wanted to see the premises they chose.

He nodded as though he approved. "We can see what renovations we want done in the home down there, too. You'll want a hand in that." I agreed. The old manor house had been rented for years by a couple who ran it as a country bed and breakfast. Now that they'd retired, Rafe had decided to spend more time there, especially as Gran and Sylvia would be living there.

"Is the housing situation there as good as it is here?" I

asked him. In the tunnels beneath my shop in Oxford, the vampires had created the most incredible underground complex of apartments decorated with the treasures they'd been collecting for centuries. I was worried that Gran and, more particularly, Sylvia, would balk if the Cornwall place wasn't as luxurious.

"Don't worry," Rafe said. "Sylvia's been there before. She'd never have agreed to move if she didn't approve of her new home. One of the reasons I bought the property was because it contains an abandoned tin mine. The complex is every bit as nice as what they've got here."

That was a relief. I was about to ask more when my phone rang. I was kind of surprised. I couldn't imagine anyone would be so rude as to phone me on the morning after my wedding. I glanced at the call display, and it was my mother. I supposed if there was anyone I could have expected would call me on this special day, it would be her. I contemplated not answering it, but she was my mom. I clicked my mobile to take the call.

"Hey, Mom, what's up?"

I could tell from her first word that she was agitated. "I'm sorry to bother you, Lucy. Your father told me not to call, but I didn't know what else to do."

I could hear voices behind her, and it sounded like she was outside. I glanced at the ormolu clock sitting on the fireplace in the dining room. It might be hundreds of years old, but it kept perfect time. Rafe made certain of it. They should be heading off punting soon. And I suddenly felt a wash of anger. I had a terrible feeling those stupid punt boats hadn't shown up or everybody was being asked to pay extra or some hideous thing. Maybe Con wanted a bribe for setting the whole thing up. "What's happened?"

"Your father's getting very agitated. We're at the meeting place on the river, but there's no one here from the punting company." She dropped her voice. "I can see lots of punts going by with proper outfits. I'm not sure this one is quite as legit as your father believed it was. He even went round to the house where they keep the punts. Everything's locked up, and there's no one here. There's no sign of Connor."

Why was I not surprised? I'd had a bad feeling something would go wrong with this "deal" that Tina's date had arranged. I thought quickly. "What about Tina? Maybe she knows where he is."

My mother's words came short and sharp like she was holding her anger in check. "I asked Tina. She says Connor left the wedding with Jennifer last night and she hasn't seen him since."

"My bridesmaid Jennifer?"

I wasn't sure of a lot of things in life, but I was sure of one thing. There was no way Jennifer had gone home with Connor. She'd been one of the last people to leave last night. I was about to say so when she said, "Jennifer hasn't turned up either."

No doubt she'd slept in or something. "What do you want me to do?"

"I don't know," she wailed. "It's actually horrible. I've got about twenty people hanging around waiting to go punting and no punting boats."

I was about to suggest they go to one of the proper companies that operated out of Oxford, when Rafe said, "Tell her we'll be right there."

I was quite surprised. "Hang on, Mom."

I looked at him. "You want to go punting?" Okay, it was an overcast day, but still. I couldn't imagine Rafe would enjoy being out in an open boat.

He shook his head. "I want to have a word with that Connor myself. We'll go out, we'll get this punting sorted out and then come back. Well, you can stay and float around on the river if you want to."

In truth, I would love to go punting one day. But not today. "Are you sure you don't mind?"

"No. I want to go." He didn't sound like he was all excited about seeing more of my relatives, so I felt there was something else going on. I told my mom we'd be right there, and she sounded more than relieved.

"Keep them busy for half an hour," I said. "Buy them coffees or Pimm's or something. We're on our way."

I ended the call and looked at Rafe. "What's really going on with you? Why do you suddenly want to go and see the punters?"

For the first time this morning, he looked quite grim. He stood up. "I didn't want to tell you. At least not yet."

"Tell me what?" I was getting a bad feeling about this.

I got up too and followed him when he beckoned. We went into the room where he kept his gallery of paintings. I took a quick glance around, but everything looked perfectly in place. However, he strode toward one of the panels that cleverly reversed to reveal the true depth of his art collection. He spun it around, and my dread increased, as I didn't really think he'd brought me in here to admire his Old Masters. As the panel clicked into place, I could see the space. In pride of place in the very center of that panel that featured the newly cleaned Rembrandt, the DaVinci drawings, and a couple of lesser-known renaissance artworks was a blank space where a painting was clearly missing. I walked closer until I was standing right beside Rafe.

"Once I saw the photo of an unauthorized visitor entering into the off-limits part of the house last night, I felt the need to check on my paintings. I did that this morning when you were outside retrieving your crystal ball."

I hated to ask, but I had to know.

"What's missing?" I didn't know his collection as well as he did, obviously. Though I had a terrible feeling I knew the answer.

He glanced down at me, his eyes coldly furious. "The Elizabethan portrait."

CHAPTER 5

"No!" I'd known it had to be bad but not this bad. "The one Queen Elizabeth gave you herself?"

"The very one. I can't tell you how much that painting means to me, Lucy. Its value is so much more than monetary. To me it's priceless."

"Then we'll get it back," I told him. I felt the hollow thud of guilt in my belly. Somehow, I was certain this was my fault. I was the one who'd wanted to get married here. And I was absolutely certain none of Rafe's friends, alive or undead, would ever do something like this. But some of my relatives? The word dodgy sprang to mind.

Now I put two and two together. "Do you think Connor had something to do with this?"

He shrugged. "Seems the obvious connection, doesn't it? That photograph showed him wandering into this part of the house where there was no reason for any wedding guest to be."

"And now he's not shown up for the punting."

"If and when he does arrive, I'll want to have a few words with him."

I put my hand on his arm. "You won't do anything you'll regret, will you?"

"That depends on what I find out. If that young thug has marred that painting in any way..." He didn't end the sentence, and I was just as glad he hadn't.

"I'll get William to come with us," he said.

"Why?" I thought William could use a day off after organizing that amazing wedding yesterday, but Rafe said, "He's very useful in difficult situations. Much better than I am. He calms people down."

I knew exactly what he meant. William was someone you could always count on. Also, I felt it would be good to have him with us in case Rafe got into it with Connor. William had a lot more experience dealing with Rafe and hopefully could prevent him from going all bloodthirsty and ragey on the guy.

One thing I was certain of, I wouldn't leave Connor and Rafe alone. Not for a second. I was as absolutely determined as my husband to get that painting back, but we'd do it in a way that left Connor with his life force intact.

A jail term, however—that I could get behind.

WHEN RAFE and I arrived at the designated meeting point for the punters, I was astonished. We followed the directions, which took us down a wooded path along the Cherwell River and ended up in a field with an old shack that might once have been a boathouse. There were no punting boats and still no Connor. Out on the river, I could see and hear people having fun, laughing, pushing the long poles into the water. There were families with children and dogs, couples, a group of laughing women that had to be a hen party. And here was a group of people who had been promised a punting trip, with no punts. I said to Rafe, "There isn't even a dock."

I saw my dad holding court, doing his best to entertain people.

He was like a tour guide, albeit an amateur one, but I had to give him credit. He was doing his best. I overheard him say, "You know, the history of punting goes back to Victorian times. It was considered fashionable for ladies to indulge. Some of the boats still operating are more than a hundred years old. Why, Susan and I spent many a happy afternoon with me punting and her reading to me." Knowing them, she wasn't reading love sonnets. She'd have been reading from a dusty archaeological textbook. "They say J.R.R. Tolkien was a keen punter." I could feel my poor father dragging up every bit of random knowledge as he waited for rescue. The guests who were listening looked politely bored.

My mother hovered on the outskirts looking anxious and miserable.

My cousin Tina sat on the grass looking thoroughly bored and hung over. She'd swapped the red dress for denim shorts and a tight tank top. She was picking the nail polish off one of her fingernails. I was about to go up to her and ask if she had any idea where Connor might be when Jennifer appeared, walking down the path towards us. I knew that Connor hadn't gone home with her, but I saw Tina glare at her, and her posture stiffened as though waiting for Con to show up with my bridesmaid.

Jen looked surprised to see us there. "Lucy? Rafe? What are you doing here?"

I quickly filled her in on the missing punts and the equally missing Connor. I wasn't sure whether Rafe wanted her to know about the theft, so I didn't say anything. But in a low voice, he told her about the theft in a few sentences. I was glad and kind of honored that he was treating my best friend with the same trust he showed me.

She looked horrified. "I am so sorry." And then she glanced at me. "We'll find him. And we'll get that picture back."

I loved that she was on our team so vehemently. "Yes," I agreed. "We will."

She said, "Connor was drinking pretty heavily last night. Maybe he slept in."

"If he's stolen my portrait, I doubt very much we'll be seeing him today."

The words "or ever" hovered in the air, but knowing the combined powers of a very motivated five-hundred-year-old vampire and two pretty well-motivated witches, I didn't think there was much chance that we weren't going to find Con the con man one way or another. We just had to get to him before he sold that painting. With luck, he'd be stupid enough to try to fence it, and Rafe's network was comprehensive enough that he'd get notified long before anyone else had a chance to buy it. I was really hopeful that this would happen and soon.

Rafe turned to William. "You go to one of the proper companies and pay whatever you have to to get a punting tour organized in the next half hour."

"Chauffeured punts?"

He glanced around the straggling group of wedding

guests, in various shapes, ages, sizes, and fitness abilities. "Yes. Definitely."

"I'll take care of it." And the amazing thing about William was, even though it was a beautiful day in Oxford and the river was already crowded with punts, I knew he'd manage it. He'd somehow have punts and guides for twenty-five people within thirty minutes.

I found my mother and told her the good news. She heaved a huge sigh of relief. "Thank you so much, Lucy."

"Don't thank me. Thank Rafe."

She beamed at her son-in-law. "Oh, I do. And please accept my apologies. I really thought we'd done a good thing." She was so upset, she was near tears.

Rafe reassured her. "You planned a lovely outing. Someone you trusted let you down. It happens. But I think we've got it sorted out now."

He was so kind to her, my heart warmed. She said, "As soon as your father finishes his latest anecdote, I'll let him know."

That done, I turned to find Tina, who was staring at Jennifer with dislike. Oh, this was going to be fun. I squared my shoulders and went over to where she sat. There was a tiny streak of bright pink nail polish left on her thumb, and she was still worrying at it.

"Tina," I said. "What happened to Con?"

She glared at me. "Ask her," she said and jerked her head at Jennifer. "He went home with her. I saw him."

Jennifer said, "No. He didn't. He took me out to where the cars were parked to show me his Jensen Interceptor. He was so proud of it, and I kind of like cars. But that's all. I came back inside. I didn't see him again."

"What time was that?" I asked.

If we were going to find the painting, and if Con had stolen it, we'd have to put together a timeline. No doubt he'd lured my friend out to the car park with him, as who would ever suspect a guy who was hitting on a bridesmaid to have stolen goods on him? For a guy who hadn't struck me as very smart, I had grudging respect for that ruse. I really doubted Connor had chosen the Elizabethan portrait knowing its value. No doubt he grabbed the first one that would fit in his pocket. He'd walked away with a fortune so easily, it made my teeth grind in frustration. Lochlan was right. Why hadn't we had better security?

And then guilt reared its ugly head again. Because for Rafe and his friends, he hadn't needed it. It was one of my guests that had caused the trouble.

I was not a violent woman, but I could have smacked Tina right then for her bad taste in wedding guests and for her rudeness to my best friend. However, as Gran had always instilled in me, you catch more flies with honey than you do with vinegar. So I forced myself not to smack her.

Jennifer was still thinking. "It must have been about eight."

"All I know is his car was gone when I left at nine," Tina said, glaring at Jennifer as though she didn't believe a word she said and she had Connor tucked away in some love nest somewhere. As if.

"How did you get back to the hotel then?" I asked Tina. She and her parents were in a suite in a hotel in Oxford that Rafe was paying for. He'd insisted on providing rooms for the out-of-town guests. I did have some sympathy for her being angry, but she was angry with the wrong person. For Connor to go off and leave her, when she was wearing those impossible shoes, must have been torment for her.

"I got a ride." Then she looked mortified. "With my parents."

"Have you heard from Connor since last night?"

"How could I? Haven't got my phone, have I? It's why I came here. Tell him exactly what I thought of him. Maybe push him in the river."

Yep, still the same old Tina I remembered well from childhood.

Then Tina glared at me, which was at least a break for Jennifer. "Besides, I don't know what you're being so high and mighty about. Somebody stole my phone at your wedding."

I said as calmly as I could, "I'm sure you just put it down somewhere. The cleaning staff are finishing the tidying up today. I'm sure it will turn up." In fact, if I hadn't been in such a rush to get over here, I might have brought her phone with me. But I didn't think it would hurt my cousin Tina to do without for a few more hours. Maybe it would be a lesson in following the rules in the future, though I doubted it.

I could tell she was getting ready to lay into me when Tina's father came staggering up from the other direction. He was red in the face, clutching his chest and panting like an unfit man who's run up a hill. He said, "I think there's been an accident."

"Oh, Dad's so embarrassing," Tina muttered. "He must have gone into the bushes for a wee."

I didn't think the accident he was referring to was wetting his pants. That man looked seriously alarmed. Then he pointed behind him. "In the river. Over there." He was gasping as though he'd run too far, and Tina's mother, my mother's cousin Ruth, went to him. "It's all right, Colin. Just take a breath."

I glanced up and caught Rafe's gaze, and then Rafe and I and Jennifer immediately began moving in the direction he'd pointed. The path was narrow at this part of the river with lots of overhanging trees and leafy bushes edging the river. Colin wouldn't have gone far, so I kept my eyes scanning left and right as we walked quickly down the path.

After only a couple of minutes of walking, I saw a wooden punting boat bumping gently against the bank. It would have been hidden from the river, and if we hadn't been walking down this particular path, we wouldn't have seen it either. As I moved closer, I felt the heaviness in the air. Jennifer and I exchanged a glance, and I knew she felt the same thing.

Rafe took the lead and pushed through the undergrowth to reach the boat. We followed.

I knew it was Connor the minute I saw the body sprawled across the boat.

CHAPTER 6

*E*ven though I couldn't see his head, I recognized the outfit he'd been wearing at the wedding yesterday, black trousers and white jacket. I also recognized the ring on his finger. He had fallen forward, and his head and shoulders disappeared over the side of the punt. Rafe deftly stepped onto the back of the punt. It rocked slightly as he peered over the side. He glanced back at me. "His head's beneath the surface of the water. He must have drowned."

I knew that there was no discussion needed about administering first aid. He'd be able to sense that there was no blood moving in that body, while both Jennifer and I sensed death.

Still, Rafe knelt and ran his hands over the body. Though he didn't lift the head out of the water. I noticed a bottle of what looked like whiskey had rolled against one of the wooden seats. The bottle was half full. Or half empty, depending on how you looked at it. I had a strong suspicion the other half was inside Connor. A wooden punting pole lay half on the punt, the rest snagged in the bushes. As Rafe rose,

I pointed out the bottle. "He must have drunk himself into a stupor and fallen and hit his head," I said.

"Strange place to sit drinking alone," was Rafe's reply. And a fair point.

"Connor wasn't the type to drink alone," Jennifer said from behind my shoulder. "I bet someone was with him. He was coming on to me hard. I remember he suggested a moonlight boatride which I assumed was a euphemism for come back to my place. I went as far as going to look at his hot car with him, but when I obviously wasn't going to leave the wedding reception with him, he moved on. I wonder if another woman said yes."

"Then where is she?" I asked.

"I don't know." She took a step closer. "But if she shared that bottle of whiskey with Connor, then the police may be able to track her from her DNA, if they decide to find her."

"Ooh, good point," I said. And not to be outdone by my best friend in the sleuthing department, I added, "And they might be able to find out where he bought that bottle. With CCTV footage and so on, that could help track his movements."

"CCTV won't help," Rafe said, stepping back off the boat to join us. "I recognize that whiskey. It's from my collection. And very expensive whiskey it is."

"You mean Connor Townes stole a bottle of your whiskey?" Jen sounded pretty surprised.

"I suspect that's not all he took," Rafe said, looking down at the body.

I was about to suggest we call 999 when Dr. Pattengale came running.

"Stand back," he commanded. "I'm a doctor."

I knew there was nothing he could do for Connor Townes now, but short of explaining that a vampire and two witches had confirmed the death, there wasn't much we could do to stop him. I wasn't sure what, if any, forensic evidence was on the punting boat, but I suspected there wouldn't be much. There must be a ton of people who rented these things every day, and I doubted they got sterilized between passengers.

The pole alone must have thousands of fingerprints. It was lying beside Connor as though he'd dropped it. And as I focused on the pole, I noted a dark smudge. It could be dirt or grime or a lot of things, but I was pretty certain it was blood.

More people had arrived now: my mother and father; Scarlett and Polly, who'd decided to join the punting as, oddly, they'd never been. The doctor, after the briefest of examinations, shook his head.

"I'm afraid he's dead."

I nodded solemnly, even though I'd known it. He said, "I'll alert the authorities."

I thought it was just as well that he do it rather than me. Not knowing what else to do, the three of us turned to walk back. Then Tina arrived. She pushed her way to the front and stared, stunned, at the body sprawled in the punt.

"Not Connor," she wailed. "Not my Connor."

And then she burst into tears. Big, heaving sobs as though her heart were broken.

"I'm so sorry, Tina," I said. It was utterly inadequate, but I didn't know what else to say.

I had a feeling her feelings for Con had been a lot deeper than his for her.

The doctor made the call and then said, "Oxford CID is sending someone out." He could have saved himself the trouble of telling us. We all knew they'd send someone. You can't just leave a dead body floating around on a punt on the Cherwell River.

He stood looking at the dead man. There was something awful about leaving him with his head in the water, but clearly this was a matter for the police to investigate. Still, it was hard not to form an opinion, and the doctor certainly did. He noted, as I had, that there was a half-empty bottle of alcohol on the floor of the punt.

He shook his head. "What a sad way for a young life to end. He's still in his clothes from the wedding, so I imagine he must have come out last night. He's the young man who was organizing this punting trip, wasn't he?"

I agreed that he was.

"He probably came out last night to make sure everything was all set for today. And then, it was a lovely evening, wasn't it? Very clear and with the moon reflecting on the water, it would have been enticing to somebody who had the key to the boathouse. No doubt he decided to take a little, late-night punt when he'd have the river to himself." He was rhapsodizing now, which made it even more creepy that he was doing it over Con's dead body. Or the part of it that we could see.

"Have you ever tried punting?" he asked.

No doubt Rafe had done it many times, but I shook my head. "Never."

"It's more difficult than it looks. And the Cher"—here he looked affectionately at the river, so calm and placid—"it can be muddy at the bottom, and sometimes a pole can get stuck. He was clearly drinking, which he shouldn't have been doing while operating a punting boat, quite obviously. He was inebriated, probably wobbled, slipped, and hit his head." He sighed. "I'll be curious what the final cause of death was. But I suspect he banged his head, stunning himself, and then if that didn't kill him, most unfortunately his upper body slipped over the side and he drowned." He looked once more at the river, where the sound of laughing and talking from other punters carried to us. "Sad business. Sad business."

The doctor went very self-important and said, "I'll remain here guarding the body if you two would like to go up to where the rest of your wedding guests are milling around. I don't think they know what to do."

I nodded. It was a not very subtle reminder that all these people were here because of us. Though that wasn't quite true. It was my mom and dad who'd organized this disastrous day out, not us. Still, there was nothing we could do standing down here. My dad, who was really impressing me this weekend, was doing his best to keep everybody together and calm. Jennifer got chatting with Polly and Scarlett, and they walked back together.

Tina's mother went to her and put an arm around the sobbing woman. "I'm assuming the punting's canceled. There's nothing we can do here for that poor boy. We might as well go back to the hotel."

But Dad gently stopped her. "I believe the correct procedure is for us all to wait until the police have arrived."

"But why? It's a tragedy, but what can we do to help the police?" Ruth asked.

My dad didn't seem to know either, but he was adamant that no one should leave quite yet. I knew that was true in a murder inquiry, but I was fuzzy on the rules following an accidental death. Anyway, I could hear the sirens. Soon somebody other than my dad would be making those decisions.

I took Rafe to one side and said softly, "Did you frisk him?"

His grim expression softened. "You make me sound like a character in one of those dreadful films you like to make me watch. No, I didn't frisk him. I did check to make sure my picture wasn't hidden in one of his pockets though."

Sounded like frisking to me. "Are you sure he didn't have it on him?"

"Quite sure."

"Darn it." I was very sorry that Connor Townes was dead. But if he'd also stolen Rafe's picture, it would have been nice for Rafe to have retrieved it quietly and simply.

I knew what my new husband was thinking. If that painting wasn't here, where was it?

Rafe said, "Let's slip away. I want to have a quick look at that chap's house before there's any fuss."

I glanced up at him. "You know his address?"

"His wallet was in his pocket. I took the liberty of glancing at his driver's license, which has his address."

Smooth. "You want to break in and see if he's got your painting."

"I wouldn't have put it that crudely, but essentially yes."

I glanced around. I wasn't sure we should leave. Maybe my dad was right. And then Rafe said, "We were never meant to be here. This was an event organized by your mother and father for other wedding guests, not the bridal couple."

He was right, of course, and no one was paying us any attention. It would be very easy to slip away. I nodded, deciding not even to say goodbye. He said, "We can continue down this way. I know this area well. We'll wend our way back to the car." Sounded like a good plan, so I walked with him down the path. On the way, he called William and explained the situation. Basically, he told him to forget about hiring punts and return to our wedding guests to help with damage control.

We hadn't gone far when a voice said, "Hey. Where are you guys going?"

So much for slipping quietly away. I turned to my best friend. "Jennifer, there's nothing we can do here. We weren't even supposed to be here. I really don't want to spend my very first day married hanging around at the scene of an accidental death."

Her eyes sharpened. "Was it accidental, though?"

I was shocked at her words. "Why would you think it wasn't?" A guy who should have known better and had already been drinking went out punting late at night and had more to drink. He had literally been an accident waiting to happen.

She looked a bit puzzled by her certainty as well. "I don't know. Gut feeling?" She shrugged her shoulders. "Connor Townes did not strike me as a man who would take a moonlit boat ride by himself. I'm positive there was someone else with him. I mean, he was hitting on me. When I turned him down, who else did he go for?"

She looked so pleased with herself that I assumed she was asking a question already knowing the answer.

"You were grilling Scarlett and Polly, weren't you?"

She grinned at me. "And I was successful. He was seen leaving with Georgia Montefiore."

"Are you kidding me? But she was with Liam."

"And you were too busy being the center of attention to notice that Liam was spending a whole lot more time with your cousin Violet than with his date."

"I did so notice." Even if I was the center of attention, which you're allowed to be on your wedding day.

"And is she here?" I didn't remember seeing her.

"No, she isn't," Jennifer said. "Don't you find that interesting? She was on the list. I asked your dad. She was supposed to be here."

I got a sick feeling in my stomach and glanced back to where Connor's body was hidden from view by the trees and foliage. "You don't think she's at the bottom of the river somewhere, do you?" I'd always thought punting boats looked very safe. They're flat-bottomed and meant to float, not race. And the Cherwell River isn't exactly Niagara Falls. It's as slow and sleepy as a river gets. When I thought of punting, I thought of a leisurely glide, not a catastrophe.

"I don't know. But I did find out where she lives."

"Why not just get someone to phone her?" I asked.

"I tried that. Scarlett called, but she's not answering."

Okay, I didn't really think she was at the bottom of the river, but a niggle of unease began behind my breastbone. That was never a comfortable feeling. I knew how much Rafe wanted to get to Connor Townes's place before anybody else showed up, but surely making certain Connor's late-night punting partner was okay took precedence. I glanced at Rafe, and from the set expression of his face, I suspected he was definitely more interested in his painting of his onetime boss, Queen Elizabeth, than he was about checking the health and safety of a wedding guest he probably didn't even remember.

But with the two of us looking at him, he gave in before we even argued.

CHAPTER 7

*I*t was pretty clear that Jennifer was coming with us and that our first priority was to find Georgia, who had allegedly left the wedding with Connor. I might have argued that Rafe's business was more important, but on the off chance that she'd come to a watery death too, I felt we needed to check on this woman. Especially as she had been a guest at my wedding. I really didn't want to lose another one. Rafe was smart enough to realize there was no point arguing with the two of us. I said he could go on his own errand if he needed to, but of course he didn't. He'd sacrifice a priceless portrait of Queen Elizabeth before he'd see anything bad happen to me, and we both knew it. Not that I was expecting any trouble, but trouble had a bad way of finding me.

William had agreed to stay behind and make sure everyone was looked after and got back to hotels or wherever they wanted to go. No one had any interest in a punting expedition after the gruesome discovery. He'd find his own way back to Crosyer Manor. As we walked back to where Rafe had parked the black luxury electric car, I had to ask Jennifer, "What were you even doing with Connor last night?"

She looked a bit sheepish. "You mean, why would I go out with him and look at his car?"

"Why would you give him the time of day? He's not exactly your type."

"Maybe I've changed. Maybe I like the flashy, boastful kind of man who ditches his date at a wedding to hit on another woman."

"You haven't changed that much. What made him so interesting to you?"

"I'm not proud of this, but honestly? I remembered all those stories you used to tell me about Tina. How mean she was to you. And here she was at your wedding dressed like Barbie at the disco and taking your picture when she'd been told not to. I don't know. She annoyed me. And so I decided to annoy her. It's small and mean, I know—"

"And there's a reason you're my best friend," I said, bumping hips with her as we walked along the path. We turned to look at each other, and at the very same time, we said, "I've missed you."

I said, "I wish you didn't have to go back so soon. Why don't you stay for a while? Have a visit."

"You know, I've been thinking about it. I like it here. And I've got nothing to get back to."

"Well, that's settled then."

She started to laugh. "Lucy, I'm not going to crash your honeymoon."

"Nobody's suggesting that you do. But stay in my apartment and enjoy Oxford. Violet will show you around. You can even help in the shop if you like."

"Actually, I had a long talk with Sylvia last night."

I'd been so busy I hadn't even noticed. "Sylvia Strand?"

"Yes. We were talking about her career. She was amazing."

"Have you ever seen any of her movies?" They were black and white and pretty old. I appreciated she'd been a real celebrity in the 1920s, but that was some time ago. I'd seen one of them, and even in black and white, I could see she'd been stunningly beautiful in her day. However, her acting was more of the frantic movement and dramatic facial expression variety that had gone out of fashion when the talkies came in.

"I have. Don't you remember when I took History of Film in college?"

"No. You took History of Film?"

"Ah, it was my freshman year. I didn't know what I wanted to do when I grew up. Anyway, in History of Film we watched a couple of her movies. Needless to say, she was pretty excited that someone alive had seen something she'd done, even knew who she was." I knew Sylvia's ego, and I could quite understand how she'd warm to Jennifer. "We talked about a lot of things. And she's invited me to drive down to Cornwall with her and your grandmother. I've heard Cornwall's beauti-ful, so I thought I'd go. You don't mind, do you?"

I couldn't have minded anything less. "Jen, that's a fabu-lous idea. I would love to spend more time with you. I don't know Cornwall very well either, so we can explore it together."

"But first you enjoy your honeymoon," she said quite firmly.

"Well, naturally."

By this time we'd reached the car. Rafe very politely opened the door for both of us, and then he got in. We drove to one of the big Victorian houses that had been broken up into flats that were so popular with students.

Jen said, "I'm not sure whether Georgia has a roommate or not, but hopefully someone will know whether she got home okay last night. Or even better, she might be home and just not answering her phone."

Rafe looked at the brick home. "Would you prefer I remain in the car?"

I said, "If Georgia's home, she might talk more easily to a couple of women."

He nodded. "Call if you need me." Before we were even out of the car, he'd pulled out his mobile. Knowing Rafe, he'd be getting hold of somebody, Lochlan probably, to get some help tracking down that painting. It occurred to me that he might get Lochlan or one of his employees to go to Connor Townes's residence, and then I discounted that idea immediately. Rafe would want to do that himself.

Jen and I walked across the gravel forecourt and buzzed her apartment.

A few moments went by, and then a female voice said, "Who's there?" It sounded like Georgia's posh voice.

Jennifer made sure she was looking at the peephole and said in a loud, clear voice, "It's Jennifer. From the wedding. I just came to check that you're okay."

She buzzed us in. The foyer contained a couple of bikes, mailboxes for all the suites, and a shelf covered in junk mail. We walked up a flight of stairs, and she was standing with the door open, waiting.

When she saw me, she said, "Oh, Lucy."

I tried not to look too relieved to see her looking alive and well. "I came along, if that's okay."

She looked a bit surprised, probably wondering why I wasn't with my husband on day one of our married life. I was wondering the same thing. "That's so nice of you. I'm fine. I just didn't feel up to punting today."

Even in sweats with the Cardinal College logo, she looked glamorous. "I was getting ahead on some reading for school. Do you want to come in?"

We did. The suite was nice. Not the fanciest rooms you could get in Oxford, but nice, elegant. The furniture was a bit faded but solid, like the house. There was an open-plan kitchen, living room, and then doors that must lead to bedrooms and bathroom. A cafetiere sat on the counter with the remains of her breakfast coffee in it.

She saw me looking at it and asked, "Please sit down. Shall I make some coffee?"

As we settled onto the couch, Jennifer said, "No, that's okay. I'm just really glad to see you're okay."

The other woman sat in a well-padded armchair and curled her legs under her. She looked quite wary. "Why wouldn't I be?"

"I don't know. Scarlet and Polly said you'd been looking forward to the punting. But you weren't there."

"I had a headache."

I'd imagined that I'd be doing the talking, but Jen had taken the lead on this, and I decided to let her. I would have led with, 'Hey, Connor Townes is dead, and you were the last person to see him,' but Jennifer was playing it way more subtly. I didn't know why. But I trusted Jen's instincts.

Jennifer said, "Look, we're all girlfriends. Did Connor do something to you last night?"

Georgia's jerk of surprise was so honest and instinctive

69

that I knew Jennifer had struck a chord. She glanced over at me. She took her time answering, seeming to choose her words carefully. "I think Connor would have liked to do something, but I was not interested. It ended with an awkward scene. He was drunk, so he probably won't even remember, but I really didn't want to see him today. That's the real reason I didn't go."

Jennifer said, "Tina thought I'd left the wedding in his car, but it was you." I could see how an inebriated Tina might have mistaken the two women. Both had long, dark hair, and both were tall and slim. From the back, walking away, especially if she hadn't paid much attention, she could have mixed them up.

Jen left a pause. Georgia looked embarrassed and uncomfortable. She started fussing with the drawstring on her track pants. Tying it tighter as though the pants were in danger of falling off. The activity allowed her to look down instead of up at us.

"I really don't need a lecture. Yes, I knew he was Tina's date, but he made it absolutely clear they're only friends." She shrugged. "I don't know. He was so full of plans. Said he was going to be coming into some money. He made himself sound like he was a hotshot. He was just so different from the men I meet in Oxford. College boys. I'd had a few drinks, more than I should. And I had other reasons."

I suspected Liam spending more time with Violet than with his date might have been at least one of the other reasons.

"Hey, nobody's judging. He's a good-looking guy," Jennifer said. Interesting that she'd kept him in the present tense for now.

"Yes, but I hadn't realized how much he'd been drinking. I never should have got in that car."

She got up and put the kettle on, starting to make coffee even though we'd said no. I didn't mind. I bet she made good coffee. The atmosphere was cozy, like the morning after a slumber party.

"How drunk was he?" Jennifer wanted to know.

"Honestly, he didn't seem that bad at first. And he was so proud of that car. I don't know a lot about cars, but it looked like fun, and it was a beautiful night, and the wedding was wrapping up so I thought, why not? We drove for a while, and then he suggested we go for a moonlight boat ride on the water." She laughed. "Honestly, I thought he was kidding. He seemed like the kind of guy who loved to make big plans. Where are we going to go on the water at that time of night? But I underestimated him. We drove back to Oxford, down by the river, and then we got out of the car and went for a walk. It really was a beautiful night. Then he admitted that he could take out a boat and we could go punting right now. He had the keys to the boathouse. It just seemed like such a fun idea at the time. Now I don't know what I was thinking, but last night it seemed like a great idea."

"I could imagine going along with something like that too," Jennifer said. "Weddings, moonlight, romance was in the air."

Georgia nodded eagerly. "I know. That's what I thought, too. And he was telling me how pretty I looked and saying all the right things. Anyway, he got this boat and helped me get onto it. I'd never been punting before. It seemed safe enough, and he assured me that the river wasn't even very deep. He got the pole and was pushing the boat along, but I could tell pretty quickly he didn't really know what he was doing either. A couple of times it got stuck, then after a while he said we should just float along for a little bit. There was nothing else on the water, so I didn't suppose it mattered. But then he took a bottle of booze out of his pocket."

Her posh voice faltered as though she was reliving the scene. "I hadn't even noticed he had it. It was whiskey or rum or something like that. It's one thing to drink champagne in the moonlight, but I didn't want to slug whiskey out of the bottle. I had one sip and gave it back to him. And then he kept drinking and talking about how he was going to be rich and I'd be awfully glad I knew him. He was going to take me to Atlantic City to go gambling. He had this bee in his bonnet about Atlantic City. 'Play your cards right and I'll take you with me,' he said. 'Maybe I'll buy you something real nice.'"

I got the feeling Georgia had come from a background where she'd been surrounded by nicer things than most of us grew up with. His promise of taking her to Atlantic City wouldn't have been a big draw.

She looked out of the window and then back again. "I started to get uncomfortable. He was getting drunk, and he made a really clumsy move on me, and I just thought, I don't want to be here anymore."

I was starting to get a picture in my head of a clumsy, over-amorous Connor and a woman defending her virtue. Jennifer was obviously thinking along the same lines.

She said, "So you pushed him off you? Did he fall into the river?"

Georgia looked quite shocked. "No. It wasn't that bad. I told him I was tired and wanted to go home. I reminded him we had to come back here in the morning and we should both get some sleep."

And yet here she was, safe in her own home, and Connor was still in that punting boat. What had happened?

"So what happened?" Jennifer asked her.

"He wasn't very happy, but he said maybe I'd like to go back to his place. I told him I didn't. He got up and used the pole to push the boat toward the shore. He pushed hard like he was in a temper, and then somebody called his name."

Oh, this was news. "Who?" Jennifer asked. I wondered if it was another woman. Connor Townes had obviously liked the girls.

"I don't know. A couple of men. He seemed pretty happy to hear their voices. Told me he needed to talk to them, and did I need cab fare."

"He didn't even drive you home?" Jennifer asked.

"I wouldn't have wanted him to. I climbed out of the punt onto the bank, nearly tipping myself out, and went up a narrow path to a wider path and found my way to the road. I walked home."

"And Connor was fine when you left him?"

She looked over at me sharply. It was the first time I'd interrupted the conversation. "Well, he wasn't exactly fine. He was quite drunk." Then her eyes went stormy. "Why, has he been saying something about me?"

Jennifer said, "No. In fact, Connor had an accident."

Georgia's eyes widened, and she looked from Jennifer to me and back again as though this might be some kind of joke. "Connor had an accident? What kind of accident?"

Jennifer shook her head. "A boating accident." There was a pause.

"But he's all right, isn't he?"

Jennifer shook her head again. "I'm sorry to be the one to tell you this, Georgia, but he's dead. He was found this morning in the punt."

"Dead?" She shrieked the word as though she couldn't believe it. "He can't be dead. The punt was in four feet of water. Even if he fell out, he could have simply walked to shore."

"It looks like he hit his head and fell forward, so his head and upper body ended up in the river and he drowned."

Georgia put her hand to her throat. "Oh, that's awful. And he was so happy and full of life. All excited about this big win."

"Did he tell you anything about how he was going to come into all this money?" I asked, interrupting again.

"No. I assumed he had a relative who died. Or he put some money on the right horse. Nothing about Connor Townes suggested that he'd made a lot of money through diligent hard work or a great idea."

We both nodded. We knew what she meant. She fussed around pouring boiling water over fresh coffee grounds, and soon the glorious smell of good coffee wafted through the room.

"I didn't want to see him today because it was all rather embarrassing, and I'd rather forget last night ever happened. But I wouldn't have wanted anything to happen to him. I'm shocked."

Jennifer said, "The police are at the scene now."

"Are you saying you found his body?"

"Not us but somebody in the punting party, yeah," Jennifer said.

Her hand went to her throat again. "But that's awful." Then she turned to me. "Oh, Lucy. I'm so sorry. What an awful thing to happen on your wedding weekend."

"I know. It definitely sucks."

Jennifer said, "I think the police will probably want to talk to you, since you were the last person who saw him alive."

"No, I wasn't. Those two men were."

"Right. But still, the police will probably want to talk to you, and you can tell them how much he was drinking."

She put a hand to her head, and now I thought she really did have a headache. "But this is dreadful. I don't want to get involved. I never should have gone in that car."

She glared at the two of us. "Please don't give the police my name and number."

"I don't suppose we'll have to," Jen said. "Enough people saw you getting in the car with him. I imagine they know by now."

She poured coffee and put a carton of milk and a bowl of sugar on the counter and told us to help ourselves. I didn't have to be asked twice.

She brought her own coffee over and slumped back down in her chair. "Great. Just great."

I asked, "Is there somebody you would rather didn't find out that you were off with Connor last night?"

"The man who took me to your wedding. Liam. He annoyed me, flirting with another woman all evening, and that's why I accepted a ride from Connor. I thought he'd drive me home and that would be it. It's Liam's fault I went with Connor anyway."

She nodded, looking both sad and irritable at the same time. "Now I'll be getting a visit from the police."

I drank coffee and wondered how Rafe was getting on.

After a few minutes of rehashing what we already knew, I nudged Jen. Rafe would want to get going to Connor's place.

Jennifer stood up and said, "Sorry to be the one to bring you the bad news. Hang in there."

It made me smile. Such an American thing to say.

We left, and as we crunched back across the gravel to where Rafe was parked, I said, "Do you think there's something suspicious about Connor Townes's death?"

She thought about it for a minute. "I don't know. But I decided to approach Georgia as though there was something suspicious. If it's just an accident, it doesn't matter. But if he was murdered? Then she's a prime suspect."

"Except he was still alive when she left, and those two men were probably the last people who saw him."

We'd reached the car by this time, and she pulled open the door to the back seat. "If those two men actually exist. It's a pretty convenient story, and who's going to say whether they were there or not?"

I looked at her. "You have the instincts of a detective."

She laughed. "I've been spending too much time with you."

I got in beside Rafe and turned to say, "How do you feel about a little breaking and entering?"

CHAPTER 8

Once more, the three of us settled into Rafe's car and headed out of town.

"Where are we going?" Jennifer asked from the back seat.

Rafe answered, "The address on Connor Townes's driving license is in Slough."

"Oh," she said. It meant about as much to her as it did to me.

He said, "Britwell Estate was a council estate build after WWII."

"How long does it take to get there?" Jennifer wanted to know.

"Depending on the traffic, about an hour," Rafe said.

I turned around to look at her. "Why? Did you have to be somewhere?"

Jennifer had been excited about punting, but that clearly wasn't happening. I thought she had a clear morning.

She said, "I wouldn't mind being closer to Oxford while the investigation unfolds. I want to know what happened. I didn't particularly like Connor Townes, but he was a fellow human being who died in suspicious circumstances. I feel like I should stick around to see if there's anything I can do. I thought if I hung around, I might overhear what some of the paramedics and the police had to say."

"I can see why you two are best friends," Rafe said, his tone dry. He didn't always love how involved I got in murder investigations.

"We're a step ahead of the police," I reminded her. "We talked to Georgia, thanks to you, Jen, and now we're going to Connor's home, most likely before the police get there. If they even bother. As far as anyone knows, his death was an unfortunate accident."

"I didn't want to say anything. It's not my place," Jennifer said. "But I think I saw blood on the punting pole in Connor's boat."

I was impressed that she'd noticed. "It might be grease or dirt," I said, not very convincingly.

"No," Rafe said. "It was blood." I figured his conclusion was as good as the forensics investigators.

"It still could have been an accident," I reminded them both. "He was drinking. That pole looked heavy."

"Oh, they are," Rafe agreed. "Most of the outfits use aluminum poles these days. They float and are less likely to inflict serious damage if they hit someone. A wooden pole can definitely cause an injury."

"So you agree the death could be accidental?" I wasn't set on proving Connor's death had been an accident so much as making sure we stayed open to all possibilities. Accidents did happen, after all.

"That's true," Rafe agreed, "but when you add in the theft of my painting, your accident theory is less believable."

Jennifer shared her theory that Georgia had made up her story about the two men approaching because she was the one who had killed him, probably unintentionally, while pushing him away from her.

Rafe listened to her with the same courtesy he always showed me when I was offering an idea. He said, "That's definitely possible but also doesn't explain the missing painting."

Jen started to speak, then stopped. Finally she said, sounding hesitant, "We don't know for sure that Connor Townes took the portrait."

I could tell from his grim nod that Rafe was well aware of the possibility. "He is our likeliest suspect, however. He might have been hired expressly to steal that particular painting and therefore had intended to pass it on to purchasers, or it was a crime of opportunity."

"You think he was smart enough to know which painting was the most valuable?" I had to ask.

"I don't know that Elizabeth is the most valuable, but she's the most precious to me."

Thinking about the theft as a premeditated crime was even more upsetting than believing Connor had seen a chance to steal and grabbed it. If the theft was planned, then I and my wedding had been used in a very cynical way, through my cousin Tina. "Do you think Tina's in on it?"

There was a part of me that would be quite happy to see her hauled off to jail for grand theft larceny or whatever it was called in England when you stole a priceless artifact.

"I doubt it," Jennifer said. "I don't think she's smart enough." I tended to agree with Jen. Tina seemed more like someone who'd be used as a way into Rafe's extremely private circle without her knowledge. Connor hadn't struck me as a man heavy in brains, but he might have been smart enough to use her as a decoy. What could get people's attention more than a woman wearing that violently red dress, the feathered hat, and tottering around on silver high heels? I even wondered if he was the one who put her up to taking the photographs, knowing it would cause a scene, thus putting all the attention on her and allowing him to slip into the manor house unnoticed.

I hated the thought that Connor had accepted an invitation to our wedding with the intent to steal. I would do everything in my power to find and return the missing painting, even if it meant some unauthorized snooping.

Once we drove into Britwell Estate, I could see why Rafe had sounded slightly dismissive. Not to be rude or anything, but let's just say people walking on the streets in this area didn't bear a huge resemblance to the people in Oxford. Connor and Tina would fit right in here.

Connor's home was in a row of red brick houses that looked like utility, not style, had been the mission when they were built. Of course, seeing how badly London had been bombed during the war, it made sense that the rebuilding was all about getting people housed and not so much about architectural beauty. Still, these were pretty grim-looking.

We parked a block away from Connor's place and walked back toward his house. A woman pushing a child in a stroller while talking on her mobile were the only people we passed. The child stared at us with interest. The mother probably never noticed us at all.

We got to the front door of Connor's place and paused. Obviously Connor wasn't going to be home. "Could he have a roommate?" I asked, though obviously neither of my companions could possibly know.

Rafe stood with his eyes closed for a minute and said, "There's no one inside."

Jen asked, "How are your witch skills coming along? Do you need me to open the door?" My witch skills were improving faster than my ability as a knitter, and that wasn't saying much. Still, I turned to her and said, "I have a perfectly good lock-opening spell, thank you very much." Okay, I hadn't practiced it for a while, but I was pretty sure I could still remember it.

She gave me a cheeky grin. "Well, you go first. And if that doesn't work, we'll use mine."

Rafe shook his head. "And if neither of you can manage it, I'll be in that house in less than ten seconds."

"Show-off." I muttered it under my breath, but of course vampires have extremely good hearing.

He said, "Well, you can show off the next time you tuck into a plate of roast beef and Yorkshire pudding and I can only watch you."

There was that.

I put all the effort I could muster into visualizing the lock clicking open and muttered the words I'd memorized from my family's grimoire, though it was simple enough. I felt Jen's power combine with mine as I spoke.

"To open this lock, let my wish be the key.
So I will, so mote it be."

To my enormous relief, I heard the click of the lock, and then I could simply turn the handle and walk in. Connor must have been pretty confident no one was going to break in because there wasn't much in the way of extra security. Rafe held us back and checked to make certain, but there was no sign of CCTV or any kind of a control panel for a security system. And from a quick look around, I could see why. There was nothing here to steal. Well, maybe the TV if you wanted something that took up most of your living room wall.

The interior was as uninspired as the exterior. Square rooms that led into each other. We walked straight into the living room, which also housed a dining area, and that led through a brick archway into the kitchen.

There was a mess everywhere. *Like, seriously, dude. Would it hurt to clean up once in a while?* Every drawer seemed to be open and the contents spilling everywhere. The cushions were all over the floor. Even the pictures that had hung on the walls no longer did. And then it hit me.

"We're not the first ones here, are we?"

"No," said Rafe.

A chill went over me. "Do you think they're still here?"

He shook his head immediately. "As I said, there's no one but us in the house."

I might have mocked his super senses before, but right now I was very glad to have them.

"You're sure it's been"—Jennifer turned to me—"what's that expression? Tossed over? Turned over? Ransacked?"

"Whatever you call it, this house has been thoroughly searched, and whoever did it had no concerns about leaving the place tidy," Rafe said. He held his anger in check, but I felt it. I didn't blame him. We'd driven out here hoping to find the missing painting, and it seemed we weren't the only ones looking for something Connor had hidden.

"Do you think whoever did this knows about the painting?"

"Probably." I supposed it was possible that Connor had several hidden things other people wanted enough to break into his home, but how likely was that?

I said, "Well, we're here anyway. We might as well have a look and see if they missed anything."

Rafe nodded, but he didn't look hopeful. Still, we went through the place carefully. Luckily, Rafe always carried linen gloves with him in case he was called on to inspect an old manuscript. There always seemed to be a few pairs in any one of his pockets, and sure enough, before we touched anything, he handed them to me and Jennifer.

"You're looking for a painting mounted on wood. Dimensions approximately four inches by six." Then his face kind of pinched up in pain. "Of course, he may have taken the canvas off the stretcher, in which case it would be like looking for a handkerchief."

"Not a handkerchief," I said. "It's going to be stiff with paint. More like, I don't know, a piece of cardboard? In fact, if I were going to transport it and I'd taken it out of the frame, which I never would, I'd pack it up like a photograph with pieces of cardboard on either side. Put 'do not bend' on it or something."

It was the first time he'd perked up. "Good point, Lucy," he said. "I'll start upstairs. You two start down here."

I have to say, Jennifer and I were very thorough. We turned over furniture that had clearly already been turned over and checked every cushion, the back of every painting. The truth was, it was pretty clear it had already been gone through before us. When I turned over the sofa cushions, they'd been sliced with a knife. Somebody had felt through all the stuffing just in case. Still, we did the same thing, in case they had missed the painting. But at the end of a fruitless hour, we had nothing. I'd even looked inside every one of the books on the bookcase. Luckily for us, Connor Townes was no reader. Still, neither Tom Clancy nor Stephen King was hiding any secrets.

The kitchen was also a mess. Packets of food dumped on counters, canisters rifled through. Every drawer opened and dumped, so fast-food menus, old batteries, and cutlery covered the floor. I stepped on a pair of dusty chopsticks and heard the crack as they snapped.

We'd already finished when Rafe came downstairs and simply shook his head.

He glanced out the kitchen window into a small back garden, but there was no shed, no place to hide anything. Connor Townes hadn't been a gardener. A few weeds grew on a broken concrete patio with a grimy plastic table and two chairs. Rafe went out and inspected the area anyway but didn't find what he was looking for.

The three of us left by the front door, the way we'd come in. I checked the doorframe to see if there were scratches or any evidence of a break-in, but there was nothing. Rafe followed my gaze.

"Professionals," he said succinctly.

"Professionals? But they left such a mess. I thought professionals left things so you couldn't tell they'd been there."

"This way is much quicker, and they didn't care that the search would be obvious."

"Because they knew Connor was dead?" I asked.

"Or wanted to intimidate him by letting him know they could enter his home anytime and didn't care about doing damage," Rafe said.

I wanted to be positive, and all I could come up with was, "Well, at least if it's professionals, they know what they've got. And they'll treat it with respect."

"Let's hope so. Because when I find them, I will not be treating them with respect." His tone sent a shiver through me. Every once in a while, the vampire with a bloody history peeped out. Not that I blamed him. I felt pretty bloodthirsty myself at this moment. It wasn't just a treasure to Rafe. That painting held the memory of someone he had cared for deeply.

When we got back into the car, I slumped back in my seat. "So we don't know any more than when we started."

Rafe navigated his way out of the estate and pulled smoothly into traffic. He shook his head. "That's not true, Lucy. We know several things. One, I think Jennifer's right. It looks very much like Connor Townes was murdered. And two, if someone paid him to steal that painting, he wasn't able to get it to them. So they had to come looking for it."

Jennifer was silent for a minute and then she said, "Wait a minute. Connor Townes probably never even came home last night. I mean, he was in the same clothes he'd been wearing at the wedding. And anyway, Georgia said they drove straight from the wedding to the punting place. So he couldn't have gone home first."

Rafe nodded approvingly. "Well done, Jennifer." I could see her perk up. It was always nice when Rafe made you feel like you were smart.

He said, "It was always possible that he came back to his

house after she left in order to hide the painting. There was also a chance that she was lying. We had to check."

I appreciated how thorough he'd been and felt kind of stupid that none of that had occurred to me. Maybe I was too much in bride mode. I had to get my sleuthing hat back on. Especially as Jennifer was not struggling with bride brain. It was so great having her around. It was like another member of the team.

And speaking of the team, I said, "Let's drive back to Oxford and see if there's any news."

WHEN WE GOT BACK to the scene of the clearly canceled punting expedition, none of the guests remained. There was plenty of police and forensics activity, though. The area had been cordoned off, and there were two uniforms standing, not letting anybody into that part of the riverside.

Before we got close, one of them said, "Sorry. This path is closed. You'll have to go back the way you came."

I was trying to think of something to say when Detective Inspector Ian Chisholm came walking towards us on the closed-off path. He was stripping off latex gloves.

I called out, "Ian!"

He focused on me and for a second went still and his eyes narrowed. Then he walked towards us, not inviting us towards the crime scene but walking past the two uniforms.

"Lucy. I understand congratulations are in order."

At one time there had been a budding romance between me and Ian, but it didn't ever go from bud to flower. However,

I liked him, and I knew him to be a serious and thorough investigator.

"Thank you," I said, and Rafe nodded. "Have you determined that it's murder?"

He had that cop's knack of never looking surprised even if he was. Instead he answered my question with a question. "What makes you think it was murder?"

I said, "We were among the first people to find Connor Townes dead. There was a smear of blood on the punting pole."

"It could have fallen on his head and knocked him into the water. I'm sure you also noticed that there was half a bottle of whiskey in the bottom of the punt. Doesn't take a genius to make the connection between boating at night while inebriated and a tragic accident."

Maybe I didn't know Ian as well as I knew Rafe, but I knew him. "But that's not what happened, is it?"

He said, "We're keeping all avenues open as we continue our investigation."

I said, "And yet they sent for the homicide detectives."

"The paramedics are very thorough. When they saw that smear of blood on the punting pole, it obviously raised questions, and they very properly wanted to make sure the death was thoroughly investigated."

Then he came closer. "I understand the victim was a guest at your wedding."

"Yes. Connor Townes." Though obviously they had the man's identity, I still repeated his name. "He was the plus-one of my cousin, my distant cousin, Tina. But you already know all this."

He nodded. "How did he seem to you last night?"

I said, "Well, it was my wedding. I had other things to do than worry about some plus-one who I had never even met before."

He looked at the other two and then particularly Jennifer. "Were you at the wedding yesterday?"

She nodded, and I introduced her. "Jennifer was my maid of honor. She was my best friend growing up."

He said, "Can any of you think of a reason why someone might want to harm Connor Townes?"

I didn't say anything. Jennifer didn't say anything. It was up to Rafe if he wanted the police involved in finding his missing painting. I wasn't remotely surprised when he only shook his head.

He said, "Like Lucy, I'd never met the man before."

Jennifer said, "I talked to him a bit. He seemed like he was making good use of the free bar."

Ian nodded. "Thanks for the help." But the tone of his voice suggested there was an unspoken addendum to those words. *Though you weren't any help at all.*

CHAPTER 9

*J*ennifer was staying upstairs in the apartment above Cardinal Woolsey's. I'd decided to keep it as a home away from home for visitors who preferred to be right in the center of Oxford rather than staying with me and Rafe in the manor house outside of town. Besides, if I was ever stuck in town very late, it might be convenient for me to have a place to stay. Violet, my cousin and fellow witch, had asked if I was going to rent it out, but the last thing we needed was strangers coming and going when the vampires made their home in the tunnels underneath the shop, so Jen could stay here as long as she liked.

Rafe drove down the tiny lane that led to the front door of my former home. It felt funny coming back here now that I'd packed up and moved into Rafe's manor house. It felt once again much more like my grandmother's home than mine. As we trod up the stairs, I heard voices and thought, yes, it was very much back to being my grandmother's house again. When we got upstairs to the living room, sure enough, there were Gran and Sylvia sitting on the couch gossiping and knitting away. Obviously, they had extremely good hearing just like Rafe, so the fact that they hadn't stopped gossiping meant they didn't care if we heard it. And sure enough, they were talking about how beautiful I had looked at my wedding, mostly in relation to the dress they'd made, or at least that was Sylvia's take on things. My grandmother gave me a little more credit, but Sylvia was convinced it was the dress that had made me look good and not the other way round.

"And here are the happy couple," Sylvia said. She hadn't acted professionally in ninety years, but she could still deliver a line with drama. I felt like we'd been announced. Then she caught sight of Jennifer and beamed with pleasure. "Why, Jennifer. What a pleasure to see you again."

She was so acting like the grand lady of the manor I had to remind her, "Jennifer is staying here." I didn't say, "And you're trespassing," but I hoped my silence made it obvious.

Maybe Sylvia didn't pick up on the social niceties, but my grandmother certainly did. She began to gather up her knitting. "Oh my dear, we didn't expect you back so soon. Of course, we'll go back downstairs. I should probably have a nap anyway. I was just too excited about the wedding. I couldn't sleep."

Jennifer said, "No. Please don't go. It's nice to see you."

She glanced at me, and I said, "And besides, we need to talk to you."

"Whatever's happened?" Gran looked at me closely all of a sudden. "Yesterday you were a beautiful, beaming bride. And today you look like a young woman with troubles." She glared at Rafe. "You haven't done something to put her off marriage already, have you?"

I hastened to reassure her. "It's not Rafe." And then I sat down on the couch opposite them and, as succinctly as I could, told them the whole story of the murder and the missing painting.

Sylvia immediately got up and went to Rafe and put a hand on his arm. "I am so sorry for your loss." I didn't think my grandmother could quite understand the depth of his loss, but Sylvia certainly could. As she was quick to remind us all. "I still remember when Lucy lost my priceless emerald necklace. It wasn't the value of the gems; it was the sentiment behind them. Cartier designed that necklace expressly for me. And when it went missing, the loss nearly killed me."

The truth was that it had nearly killed *me*. There had been a second when Sylvia, who had made me wear her priceless jewelry set to a public event, where it got stolen, had almost gone full-on vampire on me. I would never forget that moment as long as I lived. Luckily, she controlled herself in an instant, but I never forgot that she could be deadly.

I walked over to see what they were working on. Gran was always delighted when I took any interest in her knitting.

She said, "It's a mosaic stitch. It's very simple, Lucy. You could do it."

I glanced at the pattern and thought the nicest thing about my grandmother was she had more faith in my ability than I had ever had in myself. The pattern looked like a maze. There were blocks where one color would go, and they seemed to run into other blocks and then paths of what I assumed was the background color. It was a little bit like how I felt about the wedding that had turned into a murder inquiry. There were all these clues and possibilities, but which were the dead ends? And which ones led somewhere?

Jennifer sat down on the other side of my grandmother and looked at the pattern. She could speak so much more knowledgeably than I could.

"I love this stitch. And that's going to be a beautiful bag that you're making." And then they were off talking knittingese. A language I still didn't speak. Well, let's just say I was in the beginners' remedial class. I did try, I really did, but me trying to be an accomplished knitter was a bit like somebody tone-deaf trying to sing opera. It wasn't that it couldn't be done; it was just that the results weren't always what you had hoped.

"I'm making the bag for you, Lucy. I thought you could keep your knitting in it."

While we talked with Gran about her knitting, Sylvia said to Rafe, "Are there any clues?"

She wasn't talking about Connor Townes's death. She wanted to know if there were clues to the theft of the painting. He filled her in on everything we knew so far, which wasn't much. She said, "Shall I call a special meeting of the knitting club this evening?"

"Yes. I can use all the help I can get to recover my painting," Rafe said.

"And maybe we can figure out who killed Connor Townes," I added, though only Jen seemed to think solving the possible murder was much of a priority.

THE VAMPIRE KNITTING club convened that night at ten o'clock in the back room of Cardinal Woolsey's Knitting and Yarn Shop.

Hester, the permanently dissatisfied teenager, was there, though she had brightened up since Carlos, a university student and vampire, had started turning up to our meetings. Hester with a crush was at least slightly less annoying than Hester when she was convinced everyone and everything was against her. I tried to be sympathetic because it must be horrendous to be permanently stuck in the teenage years, but she tried all our tempers. She was working on yet another black garment.

Silence Buggins turned up, knitting a pair of woolen stockings, as she claimed she felt the cold. I'd ordered a book of Victorian knitting patterns just for her, and she was working her way through the book, exclaiming extremely often how she'd worn this very shawl, or a doily much like this one had graced her mother's dressing table.

Dr. Christopher Weaver was knitting himself a new waistcoat. He had quite a collection. Alfred, who would accompany Gran and Sylvia to Cornwall, was trying his hand at a Cornish fisherman's sweater. When Hester asked if he was going to take up fishing in Cornwall, he looked down his long nose at her and said, "Perhaps," in a cryptic way as though he had secret business we could know nothing about.

Naturally, that caused Hester to heave a huge sigh and say, "Fine, don't tell me what you're up to. I don't care. No one invited me to go to Cornwall, so you can just shove off."

Gran, who was the nicest of the vampires—and I didn't only think that because she was my grandmother—looked up from her mosaic work. "Do you want to come to Cornwall, dear?"

Alfred scoffed. "What's Hester going to do in Cornwall? She's putting on airs to be interesting."

I could sense a blowup in the air the way sailors can smell a storm coming. I had no idea how to avert it, but Carlos leaned over to Hester and asked if she could help him with a tricky part of his knitting. She'd been teaching him to knit, and his timely question saved us from an emotional tirade. I could have kissed him, except that would have set Hester off again.

I settled myself beside Theodore, who was crocheting a cushion. He whispered to me that it was going to be a gift for Gran, for her new home. I thought that was a lovely gesture.

Gran had nearly finished the mosaic bag she'd begun only that afternoon. Sylvia was knitting herself a new dressing gown in gray and silver.

Reluctantly, I'd brought some knitting along too. Frankly, I'd have thought one of the nicest things about being on honeymoon would be that no one would expect me to knit anything. However, as usual that turned out not to be true.

My latest project was a baby blanket for Alice and Charlie's baby. I figured I had at least six months to complete the blanket, and it was a very simple project done in garter stitch in a pretty pale green. I pulled out my tangled mess and poked at it as though it were a wilting plant I might revive. After watching me for a few seconds, Theodore very gallantly untangled the mess I'd made and reknit my stitches up to where I'd left off. I sent him a pathetic look, and he rapidly knit a few more rows for me, then handed the work back to me. "It's important you don't let others do too much for you," he said softly.

"Define too much," I requested.

He shook his head at me. "Lucy, as the proprietress of a knitting shop, don't you want to become proficient?"

"Proficient? I certainly do aim for it." Sometimes it felt like I was aiming at the moon with a bow and arrow.

Theodore was allowed to say words like proprietress because when he'd been alive, women hadn't worked outside the home unless they were servants, so I gave him leeway with his old-fashioned language.

Jennifer had one of the Cardinal Woolsey's bags, and from it she pulled the newest issue of Teddy Lamont's knitting magazine and a couple of balls of wool. She saw me looking and said, "I'm excited to try this sweater. Isn't it gorgeous?"

It was. A sweater designed with impressionist flowers in purples and blues. It would be wearable art. I was smitten with envy for Jen's talent. *Please let her not decide to make Alice's baby a blanket.* I told her the colors would look great on her, and we settled to work.

Rafe had a bag of knitting with him, but Lochlan hadn't bothered to bring anything to work on. I suspected they planned to run the investigation part of the meeting.

I wasn't very surprised when Lochlan came in followed by Guy, the young vampire who, dressed as a waiter, had fallen out of the window at my wedding. Needless to say, you'd never know he'd been defenestrated just over twenty-four hours ago. He looked as hale and hearty as someone of his pale complexion could look.

"I'm sorry, I don't knit," he said, sounding apologetic as he glanced around at the industrious vampires.

"How do you pass the time?" Gran asked him.

"I work for Lochlan," he said. "And I play a lot of video games."

"You should try knitting, for some variety," Gran

suggested. "The shop you walked through belongs to Lucy. She'll be happy to ring up a purchase if you'd like to get started tonight." I wasn't sure if Gran was genuinely trying to help a fellow vampire or create a new long-term customer for the shop. Both, probably.

He looked unsure and said, "Thanks. Maybe later."

Rafe called the meeting to order and briefly filled in everyone who didn't already know on all the details of the suspicious death of Connor Townes. He also shared with this group what he hadn't shared with the police, that a valuable painting had been stolen from his private collection. This caused a lot more furor among the vampires than the suspicious death, frankly. I mean, you had to figure they'd seen a lot of human death in their time, caused quite a bit of it. However, somebody stealing a sentimental and irreplaceable possession, something from an earlier time in history—that got their attention. Every one of them felt the pain of that loss.

"He won't get away with it," Silence Buggins said. Silence was a genius at both stating the obvious and talking way too much for somebody with her name. It was a cosmic joke that anyone thought Silence was a good name for that baby.

"Do you have any leads on where the painting might be?" Theodore asked. Theodore had a round baby face and the most innocent look you've ever seen, but behind it was a steel-trap mind. He'd been a police officer in life, and now he ran a private detective firm.

Rafe shook his head. "I believe Connor Townes stole the portrait. My instinct is that if we can solve Connor Townes's murder, we might get closer to finding my Elizabeth. I believe he was killed for it."

I really hoped he was right. I wanted to get that painting back as badly as anybody. If someone had killed Connor to get the portrait, then solving Connor's murder should lead us to the thief.

That was the theory, anyway.

There was a whiteboard in my back room that had come in quite handy for drawing out big-picture scenarios. Sometimes I used it for my business. I'd think about all the ways I could increase my newsletter or bring more business to the online part of the shop. This was becoming a pretty significant part of my little business. However, I'm sad to say, more often than not we used that board to help solve murders. If real life was remotely like television cop shows, the police did the same thing.

The police had considerable resources at their disposal, but frankly, so did we. Rafe never revealed his sources, but he had contacts in all kinds of strange places. Honestly, I never realized how many vampires were walking around hiding in plain sight, just like the rest of us, only slightly pale. And Oxford was a perfect place to hide. He refused to say how many of the dons were undead, but looking around at the college teaching staff did make me wonder. It would explain how they got to be so smart and had such a wealth of knowledge. I mean, in one lifetime, you can only learn so much. But over a hundred lifetimes? Two hundred? So long as you could retain what you'd learned, your breadth of knowledge in history would be amazing, as I saw every day in my husband.

It could be very intimidating being around so much experience and knowledge. However, what I believed I had, and Jennifer had, that they didn't have was what you might call a fresh perspective. Maybe we'd only been around for thirty years as opposed to three hundred or five hundred or eight hundred, but we were a little better in tune with the lives and attitudes of younger living people today. And, of course, Connor Townes had been a lot closer to our age than to anyone else in this room. Okay, it wasn't much of an edge, but it was something.

I had discovered something I didn't remember about Jennifer before. She was tenacious, and did I sense a hint of competitiveness in her?

If I was really honest with myself, did I notice a slight rise in my own urge to get a few "well done, Lucy's" or even to solve the case? I didn't like to delve too much into my own darker side, but I suspected there was indeed a friendly rivalry between the two of us. Sisterly, I suppose you'd say, as we were both witches. It would never get in our way, we'd both make sure of that, but I didn't think it was a bad idea for us both to be just slightly competitive with each other.

I'd have to see how that went.

Anyway, there we were, and while the vampires, Jennifer, and I knitted, crocheted, or pretended to do one or the other, Rafe and Lochlan had a soft-voiced conversation at the edge of the room. Then, to my surprise, it was Lochlan who went up to the whiteboard and gazed over at us in a way that, without even uttering a word, commanded complete silence. Rafe had that ability too. They'd been alphas in life, and they were definitely alphas in the afterlife.

He said, "Good evening. I think you all know me, but for anyone who doesn't, I'm Lochlan Balfour. I had the privilege of being Rafe's best man at his wedding, and what little security there was at Crosyer Manor yesterday," and here he shot a quick glance at Rafe, "was provided by me and my company. Therefore, I'm mortified to discover that a valuable painting went missing from Rafe's home. Now I know some of you were there yesterday, and it's my intention to gather what clues we can. Did you see or hear anything that might help us track down a valuable work of art?"

Guy, the vampire/security guard/waiter, looked incredibly uncomfortable, like somehow it was all his fault. Rafe obviously noticed his discomfort too, for he said, "If anyone's at fault, Lochlan, it's me. I was arrogant enough to believe that my own skills and that of the staff I employ was enough to safeguard both my privacy and my valuables. Clearly I was wrong."

Lochlan nodded. "Well, blame is futile at this point. Let's get that painting back."

Jennifer spoke up then and said, "While I completely support you wanting to get Rafe's property back, let's not lose sight of the fact that a man died last night."

She simply wasn't used to being around vampires the way I was. I could see them looking at her thinking, "Right, guy died. Never seen that happen before." While the theft of a painting that had huge sentimental value, that they could get worked up about. And it wasn't like it was a human they'd even known. Connor Townes was exactly the kind of person who would have been vampire bait in the years before blood products became so readily available. Modern vampires didn't need to hunt unless they wanted to, and I was happy to say that none of my friends wanted to. They'd embraced a more civilized way of living. But in an earlier time, Connor would have provided a nice meal.

In the pause where a couple of vampires nodded and most of them just kept knitting, Lochlan said, "Thank you,

Jennifer. That's a very good point." And then he looked at Rafe. "Do we have any more information about the demise of the unfortunate Connor Townes?"

Rafe nodded. He was working on a cashmere scarf in navy blue, and he put down his work. Then he rose and addressed the group. "I don't think the police are quite sure whether the death of Connor Townes was accidental or deliberate. Here's what we do know. There was a massive blow to the back of his head, a bloody mark on the punting pole, and his lungs were full of water, which suggests the cause of death was drowning but clearly precipitated by the stunning blow. The question is, was that blow accidental or deliberate?"

"Doesn't it seem likely that he was hit on the back of the head from behind with the punting pole?" Theodore asked.

"That's certainly a possibility, but his blood alcohol level was elevated to a toxic degree. It's entirely possible the pole fell on his head and knocked him into the water."

Jennifer looked horrified. "That can happen?"

"Yes. A wooden punting pole is heavy. If he propped it up and wasn't paying proper attention, it could easily have fallen on him."

"Punting always looks so peaceful in the movies," Jen said.

"You'd be surprised by the benign-looking things that can kill a person," Rafe said.

"Bee allergies," Alfred said, pausing in his knitting and looking down his long nose at the rest of us. "I once watched a young man picking a bouquet of daisies for his sweetheart. He didn't know he was allergic to bees until it was too late." He shook his head. "Blood type O. Such a pity. O is so common." He stuck his tongue out a little way as though tasting something unpleasant.

"Anyway," I said brightly, "we don't know any more than we did earlier. Connor Townes could have been killed, or it could have been an accident."

"Not so fast, Lucy," Rafe said. "The police have discovered his background is rather unsavory."

Why was I not surprised that my cousin Tina would pick an unsavory character for her date to my wedding? Another mark against cousin Tina.

Theodore, the former cop and currently a private eye, said, "Can you be more specific about *unsavory?*"

"The investigation is obviously only beginning, but he's been arrested several times for theft, did a few months behind bars at one point, and runs with a group of louts with similar backgrounds to his. They're notorious thieves and fences, and one of them runs the punting company from his great-aunt's property near the river. Jason Smith."

I said, "That ties in with what Georgia Montefiore told us. Two men called out to Connor last night. It makes sense that it could have been this Jason Smith and another of the thieves and fences Connor liked to hang with. They could have killed him and taken the painting." Though that didn't explain why Connor's home had been turned over by someone obviously looking for something.

Theodore nodded. "Do Connor Townes or these associates have any connection with the world of art theft? That is a refined area where you get a much better class of criminal."

While I had to hide my smile against such unconscious snobbery, what Theodore said made sense. Connor looked like the kind of guy who'd steal the hubcaps off your car when you were sleeping, slip the wallet out of your purse when you were looking the other way. The kind of guy that would get you a good deal on punting that was both a terrible deal and included a nice fat kickback for himself. But was this the guy you'd hire to steal the Mona Lisa? I didn't think so.

Obviously, I wasn't the only one in the room having that thought. Sylvia said, "Are we certain there's a connection between the death of this unfortunate young man and the theft of your painting?"

CHAPTER 10

"*E*xcellent question, Sylvia," Lochlan said, regaining control of the meeting. I wondered if there was a kind of friendly rivalry between him and Rafe the way I sensed one developing between me and Jennifer. Rafe, seeming happy to let Lochlan reclaim the lead, retired back to his knitting. He looked perturbed. "We just don't know."

Sylvia said, "And that's where we come in. Those of us who were at the wedding. Or you, Agnes. You had a bird's-eye view from up there. It must have been like a chessboard to you. Did you notice this Connor Townes sneaking into the house and coming out carrying something about the size and shape of a painting?"

Did she mean to be sarcastic? I wasn't sure. Gran didn't seem to take it that way. She looked over at me and smiled.

"I'm terribly sorry, but I spent the whole time looking at Lucy. And didn't she look lovely in that gown? I do think we outdid ourselves."

All the vampires who'd had a hand and a couple of needles in the creation of my gown nodded, looking rather pleased with themselves. I took that moment to thank them once again.

"Honestly," I said, "I felt like a princess."

"And you looked like a queen," Rafe said.

There was a moment that just shimmered with goodwill, when Lochlan broke the spell, saying, "And speaking of queens, we have a missing painting of one that we're trying to find."

Right. Everyone got serious again. Gran, clearly wanting to be helpful, said, "I did see Connor speaking to Lucy at one point. And he also spoke to you, Jennifer. And while I have to say your dress wasn't as spectacular as Lucy's, you not being the bride, you made a most beautiful bridesmaid."

"I agree," Sylvia said. "I've always had an eye for fashion. And if one looks at a wedding as though it were a stage, of course the secondary actress's costume should always echo back and amplify that of the star."

I loved this. In three minutes I'd been called a princess, a queen, and a star. None of those were true, but if a woman can't be all those things on her wedding day, when can she?

I could see that Lochlan was quickly running out of patience with talks of wedding gowns and stage and screen stars. I said, "I did talk to Connor briefly, Gran. But mostly we were talking about my cousin Tina."

Here Gran shook her head. "If I'd still been alive, I would have talked your mother out of that terrible idea of inviting that young woman. She was always trouble. And jealous of you. The times she'd steal your toys or eat your cake as well as her own, and then call you a baby when you cried, are past counting."

Okay, we'd moved away from me being a princess, a star,

and a queen to me being a big crying baby. That didn't take long. Next someone would start criticizing my knitting, and I really would turn into a big crying baby.

My gaze fell to Gran's knitting. I said, almost without thinking, "This case is a bit like your knitting, Gran. Like a mosaic. I'm looking at the pattern, but you've got dark lines running here and pale lines running there, and I have to ask, where's the pattern here?"

Lochlan, surprisingly, seemed quite taken with my random comment. He walked over to Gran and said, "Do you mind?" and opened his hand for her to hand him her work. She quite happily did. He walked back in front of us, and he pulled out a strand of the blue wool and a strand of the yellow. It was a lovely dramatic moment, and he had us all paying attention. Everyone stopped knitting to see where this was going. He pulled at the blue strand. "This is Lucy and Rafe's wedding, culminating in the theft of the painting." With his other hand he pulled the piece of yellow yarn taut. "And this is the death of Connor Townes. Do these threads connect?" He pulled them together and looped the colors together. It was quite a dramatic visual aid. And then he unwound them and separated them again. "Or are they two completely unrelated incidents?"

"That seems like the first thing we need to determine," Theodore said.

Lochlan nodded. "Theodore, in your profession as a private investigator, can you follow up Connor Townes's criminal connections? Is there a hint of him being an art thief or having any knowledge or connection with fences in the art world?"

Theodore looked quite gratified to be given such an important job. He nodded, "Of course. I'll get right on it."

Jennifer said, "But if Connor came to steal the painting, how did he even know it was there? Somebody must have hired him to do it."

"Unless it was a crime of opportunity," Dr. Weaver said.

"But how would he even know to go and look behind those panels to where you keep your real treasures?" Sylvia asked. "I don't believe you share that information with too many people."

"I don't," Rafe said with feeling.

"But someone knew," Lochlan said. "Even if it was simply a crime of opportunity, someone had to know that portrait was there." He turned to Rafe. "Who at your wedding knew about the panels?"

Rafe put down his knitting and thought carefully. "You, of course." He glanced around the room. "Is there anyone here who didn't know?"

Hester let out a groan like this was the most boring meeting she'd ever attended. "Well, I probably did, but I don't care."

Carlos put up his hand. "I did not know it. And I congratulate you on having such a lovely collection. Have you any Spanish masters I might look at? A Velázquez, perhaps?" I forgot that he was a university student and an intellectual. Hester made a sound like the air being let out of a balloon. She might be crushing on this guy, but she was not a woman who was interested in fine arts.

"I'll give you a private tour," Rafe said, obviously happy to share his collection with someone who could appreciate it.

Sylvia bristled visibly. "I hope you're not suggesting that any one of us would steal from a friend."

"Of course not," Lochlan hastened to say. "But who might have overheard a discussion? Is there anyone you might have told inadvertently? What we're trying to do is get back to the source of the leak, let's call it, if there was a leak of information."

"What about the mortals?" Sylvia asked quite sharply.

Jennifer said, "I never knew about them until last night."

Rafe said, "I rarely show mortals. William and his sister, who are my human family, naturally know all about my collection. Lucy, of course."

I looked at Rafe. "You showed my parents. Remember how excited my dad was when he saw the Van Gogh?"

"They're part of my family now, too," Rafe said. "Apart from the obvious, I have no secrets from your parents."

"Let's hope they're not the kind of people who would steal from their own son-in-law," Sylvia said. She was going to get the sarcasm award tonight, the way she was going.

The young waiter vampire said, "I knew there was something valuable in that room, but Lochlan didn't tell me what."

"Yes, we're forgetting that waiter got pushed out of the window," Alfred said. He turned to Guy. "You and the dead man were both wearing white jackets. Is it possible someone mistook you for Connor and his death was planned all along?"

"That means the murderer was at my wedding," I said, not liking this theory at all.

"And that's another thread in this complicated pattern," Lochlan said. "The attack on Guy."

He was busy at the whiteboard writing. He had two

columns, headed Art Theft and Connor Townes. And now he added a third. Attack on Waiter.

"Is the attack on Guy related to the theft?" He turned to Guy. "Did you surprise the thief up there?"

"I went up because someone sounded like they were in trouble. It was Lucy's grandmother singing. I didn't see or hear anyone else."

"And yet someone else must have been up there, in the room where you were attacked," Gran said. "I assure you I didn't push you out of the window."

"That's very kind of you," Guy said politely.

"But who did?" Sylvia asked. "I believe Guy somehow rattled the thief. If Connor Townes thought you'd seen him steal the portrait, he might indeed push you out of the window, thinking of course that you would die. It must have been very unnerving for him to discover you all but bounced."

"But who put Connor up to the theft? Or did he go snooping and get lucky?" Jen asked. We kept coming back to this question.

Gran looked at me and was almost apologetic as she said, "Lucy, I know Tina isn't your favorite cousin, never mind not your favorite person, but I do think you're going to have to talk to her and find out how she came to invite Connor Townes to your wedding."

Even as I was about to say absolutely not, Lochlan said, "That's an excellent idea, Agnes. If Tina went out of her way to invite him simply so she'd have a date to Lucy's wedding, that's one thing. Or did he, knowing she had an invitation, ask to be her invited guest? It would make a crucial difference to our investigation."

I felt completely ganged up on. I made a sound probably a lot like Hester made when she was asked to do something she didn't want to, or even worse, prevented from doing something that in her teenage heart she did want to do. Then, in a belligerent tone, I said, "Fine. I'll ask her."

"Well, you won't get anywhere if you ask her like that," Sylvia said tartly. "Jennifer, you'd better go with her and make sure she acts nicely."

My jaw dropped. What was this thing with Sylvia and Jennifer? Jennifer, who knew me as well as anyone, could obviously see what I thought of that idea. She said quickly, "Lucy's extremely adept at getting people talking. She'll do a great job without my help."

I sent her a grateful look. But Sylvia was adamant. "I remember well what it's like when a woman is jealous of one. Oh, the stories I could tell you. The starlets who would have happily ripped my heart out with their bare hands if it would have got them a role in one of my films. Torn me to shreds if they could have taken my spot on stage even for one evening. And one thing I do know about jealousy, that green-eyed beast, is that it's very easy to provoke a jealous woman. No, I think you and Lucy together would be the perfect pair to find out how Connor Townes got his invitation to Lucy's wedding."

Almost as though she were giving stage directions, she suggested where I should sit or stand in relation to Tina, and where Jennifer should, and who should say what. "You're looking to provoke her jealousy of you, Lucy, and Jennifer, you are the sympathetic ear into which she pours her imagined slights." She looked quite pleased with herself. "I've often thought of turning my talents to writing for stage and screen now I can no longer perform."

Into the stunned silence, she said, "Under a pseudonym, naturally."

Lochlan spoke again. "So Lucy and Jennifer will speak to Tina." I was actually really glad to have Jennifer's company. It would give me a buffer between me and the woman that I liked less every time I saw her. Jennifer glanced at me, and I gave her a tiny nod, so she agreed.

"Good," Lochlan said. "That's settled." He uncapped one of the markers. "And now we're going to try as best we can to recreate a couple of moments during the wedding."

Jennifer said, probably without thinking, "Too bad there weren't any photographs."

Lochlan said, "There were a few. Thanks to Lucy's cousin Tina breaking the rules." He reached for a black computer bag and from it pulled a fancy laptop, much nicer than anything I'd ever owned. He opened it and pulled up the photos Tina had snapped. One by one, they filled the screen.

"It really was a lovely wedding," Gran sighed.

If you didn't count waiters getting pushed out of windows and priceless art being stolen from under our noses, she was right.

He pulled up the photo that showed Connor disappearing into the house. "This is our strongest evidence that Connor Townes was the one who stole The Elizabeth," Rafe said. I loved that he called it The Elizabeth rather than just the painting.

"So it could easily have been Connor Townes who pushed you out the window," Sylvia said. "That was a bad moment, thinking poor Lucy's wedding had been ruined by death. I was very relieved to discover that you were unharmed."

"Thanks. Still wouldn't want to be falling out of windows every day, though. It hurt."

Sylvia continued, speaking to Lochlan now. "And you and Rafe were so very quick getting to the accident victim so no one else could see what was going on."

"Except the doctor," I reminded her. I still felt queasy when I thought of poor Dr. Pattengale looking so puzzled as he examined a fall victim and found him to have a very slow pulse and skin that was cool to the touch. Luckily, my father had taken him under his wing and probably fed him enough whiskey to help ease his shock and hopefully add a big dose of confusion to his memories.

Sylvia suddenly said, "You know what's odd, is that I was watching from inside the lounge, and while most of the guests were gathered in the reception area for the speeches, I'm sure the doctor arrived from a different direction."

She had all our attention now. "What direction?" Rafe asked.

"Wait!" Sylvia said and then closed her eyes. She could do anything with drama. We all waited in growing suspense. She was either recreating what she'd seen in her mind or simply making us wait to draw out the suspense. Hard to say with Sylvia. Probably a bit of both.

And then she opened her eyes. "I am almost certain he came from the closed-off wing."

"He could have just been coming back from the bathroom," Jennifer said.

"But the guests were using the bathrooms in the old stable block. He'd have had to ignore the signs and move the rope barrier," I said. Which was incredibly rude of him. I'd known the man since I was a baby. I couldn't imagine him deliberately flouting the rules.

So what was my dad's old friend doing in the closed-off part of the house?

Rafe said, "I think perhaps I'll invite the doctor and your father to a glass of brandy in a quiet bar in Oxford. Ostensibly it will be to thank the doctor for his efforts, and since he's great friends with your father, it would make sense for your father to be there too. Three men enjoying a quiet brandy. What could be more natural than to bring up a discussion of some of my treasures? Let's see if anything slips out."

I was really having a hard time picturing Dr. Simon Pattengale as an art thief for several reasons, but one immediately jumped out. "If the doctor is a high-level art thief, why isn't he richer?"

"My dear," Sylvia said with annoying condescension, "the truly wealthy never show it off."

This from a woman who drove around town in a Bentley and didn't consider herself dressed if she wasn't wearing a small fortune in jewels.

Rafe ignored her interruption, which made it easier for me to do the same. "I'm not suggesting he took the painting, but it's a line of enquiry worth pursuing."

Lochlan said, "So we've got Theodore looking into Connor Townes's associates. Lucy and Jennifer having a frank discussion with Lucy's cousin Tina about how the man received an invitation to the wedding in the first place. Rafe will find out what the doctor knew." He tapped his marker on the board. "And I will have a quiet word with some of my contacts in the art world."

Why was I not surprised he had contacts high up in the art world? He turned around looking rather pleased with himself. "In fact, I might let it be known in certain circles that I'm in the market for royal portraits. Tudors in particular."

"Yes, these are all good ideas," Sylvia said. "But what about us? Agnes and I would like a role in this investigation. And, as Lucy's grandmother, I think Agnes has earned the right."

I had to press my lips together to stop from grinning. She had such a way of putting things. However, Sylvia was supposed to be taking my grandmother down to Cornwall. We really needed to get her out of Oxford. She was struggling too much with not accidently going out in the day, forgetting that all her former friends thought she was dead. It was just too stressful.

Rafe, who'd had a few more hundred years than I to develop tact, said, "I'm so pleased you've offered, Sylvia. I've got a connection in Cornwall. And since you and Agnes are heading down that way anyway, I'd be very grateful if you could interview them."

Sylvia looked both gratified and suspicious. "You have an art contact in Cornwall?"

"Several, in fact. St. Ives is an artists' haven," he reminded her. "I'll set up a meeting and get you the details before you head off." And if I were to hazard a guess, it would be that he now had to figure out the errand.

Sylvia said, "All right. That seems like a good plan. But I've offered Jennifer a ride in the Bentley. We can't possibly leave until she's finished her enquiries."

Wily old vampire. She just didn't want to miss any of the excitement.

Rafe knew her as well as anyone. He said, "That's very kind of you to offer Jennifer a ride."

Jennifer said, "But I don't have to go. I'm happy to stay here and help."

Rafe shook his head. "No. You should go. It would be lovely for you to have a holiday. And this could be a significant part of the investigation."

There wasn't much Jennifer could say now. Two pretty forceful vampires were encouraging her to go down to Cornwall in the Bentley. If I was her, I'd have said yes as well.

I said, "We might as well talk to Tina in the morning, while she's still in Oxford and still shaken up from the news of Connor Townes's death."

I recalled the heaving sobs when she'd discovered his death. I thought that to her, Connor Townes might be more than just a useful plus-one.

But how much more?

There was a pause, and it seemed like the meeting might be over when Carlos said, "What about the river spirit?"

I stared at him. "River spirit?"

He nodded. "They joke about it in my college. Say you have to watch out for the river spirit in the Cherwell. I have never seen it, only heard rumors."

I glanced around. "There's a river spirit in the Cherwell?"

None of the vampires seemed to know anything about it. "I suppose there could be," Christopher Weaver said. Dr. Weaver had a private practice at Oxford and came into contact with students. "But I've never seen it."

There was a time I'd have scoffed at the very notion of

water deities outside of mythology, but that was before I discovered I was a witch and became friends with a group of vampires. Now I understood there were other worlds and creatures within this one. "Who would know if such a spirit exists?" Sylvia asked, snipping off a thread.

"And more important, how to make contact?" Alfred asked.

I had an idea I knew who would have that information, but I didn't want to say the name aloud.

Jennifer looked over at me. "What about the head of your coven? Margaret Twigg."

Okay, so Jennifer said the name aloud for me. In the interests of careful sleuthing, I nodded. "Margaret might know."

"Then we should go and visit her," Jen continued, either unaware or ignoring my lack of enthusiasm. What Jen didn't know was that no visit to Margaret Twigg was uncomplicated. If she wasn't trying to steal my familiar, she was making me do unpleasant tasks and nagging me about working at my craft. She was a very powerful witch, but like many powerful substances, I could only take her in small doses.

Naturally, everyone agreed that me and Jen visiting Margaret Twigg to get more information about the river deity was a great idea.

Giving in to the inevitable, I suggested we go the next day.

CHAPTER 11

I felt like I'd pulled the short straw in the job department. I didn't want to talk to Tina to find out how Connor Townes had ended up at my wedding. I hadn't wanted her there and certainly hadn't wanted him there. Now I had to spend more time with the woman to figure out how Connor had ended up coming. Had it been his idea or hers?

Equally unpleasant was the idea of visiting Margaret Twigg, and that was also on the to-do list.

However, in the interests of sleuthing, as Gran would be the first to tell me, best to get the unpleasant task done as quickly as possible and then it's over with. Which, like so many of those old-fashioned aphorisms, always sounded better in theory than in reality. At least Jennifer was coming with me.

We left the vampire knitting club meeting and, after agreeing to meet back here in the morning, she went upstairs to my old flat. It felt so strange to see her going up to what I still considered was my place. Meanwhile, I headed off into

116

the night with my new husband. "Are you disappointed that we're not on our honeymoon right now?" I asked him.

He seemed to think about it. "So long as you're with me, I don't really mind." That was such a nice thing to say. Especially since, thanks to marrying me, he was short one very important painting.

I said, "Do you think we'll ever get that painting back?"

He was silent for quite a few seconds, as if he took my question seriously. I really liked that about him. He said, "Yes. We will."

I so hoped he was correct.

It was too late to call my mother, so I put that off until the morning, along with thinking how much I didn't want to talk to Tina. I sent Margaret Twigg a message asking if Jen and I could visit her the next day, and she agreed we could come in the afternoon. She didn't sound any more enthusiastic to have me visit her than I was to go to her cottage.

"Don't forget to put your witch's globe out in the moonlight tonight," was her final message.

THE NEXT MORNING, I woke my mom to see if Tina had stayed on in Oxford. It was Monday, and no doubt she was expected to be at her job, but I couldn't imagine her leaving the day after Connor's body had been discovered. Sure enough, Mom said they were staying on at the hotel one more day and Tina was definitely staying over too. When I told her that Jen and I were going to visit Tina to see how she was after the shock of the day before, she decided to come with us and have her own visit with her cousin Ruth and Ruth's husband, Colin.

I was about to argue that this was a terrible idea but stopped myself in time. It was actually a brilliant idea. Mom could keep Ruth and Colin out of the way while Jen and I talked to Tina. I agreed to pick Mom up on the way as she and my dad were staying in a friend's Oxford flat while they were traveling.

I dressed with no enthusiasm. I picked out a summer dress with yellow daisies on it that made me happy, then thought Tina might feel it inappropriate in light of the death. So I changed to a pair of light jeans and paired it with a cashmere sweater so fine it was more like wearing a cloud than actual clothing. It was pale gray, which seemed suitably somber. I would look like a rain cloud. William made me blueberry pancakes as though he guessed I needed a treat, and that cheered me up no end.

"Are you going to return Tina's phone?" Rafe asked as I speared the last maple-syrup-drenched bite of pancake.

"I guess," I said around my bite of food. In fact, I'd completely forgotten her phone and was glad he'd reminded me.

I fetched it and put it in my bag, then brushed my teeth and swiped on some lip gloss. I thought about painting my nails or rearranging my sock drawer. Maybe moving my socks to a whole new drawer. Anything to put off seeing Tina.

However, I was a mature, married woman now. I should act like a grown-up.

So I didn't "accidentally" drop Tina's phone in the toilet.

I was definitely maturing.

≈

I PICKED up Jen and then my mother, and we headed to the hotel together. When we got to the suite Tina was sharing with her parents, we found her sitting at the table looking out of the window. She was dressed all in black. No true widow ever looked as bereft. She could have taken the whole look from Hester's wardrobe. She looked like a goth vamp or a teenager, except for the teenage part. She was around my age, and the whole widow act was a bit over the top.

She looked at us and sighed, again reminding me of Hester. "I suppose you're here to give your condolences?" she said in a breathy voice.

Since Jennifer knew me well, she took a moment to kick my ankle gently. She was the first one to speak.

"Oh, Tina, I am so sorry for your loss. I can't imagine what you're going through right now. Lucy and I wanted to come and see if there was anything we could do."

Man, she was laying it on with a trowel. Still, I was smart enough to follow her lead, as I could see how much it meant to Tina that we'd come. And, in fairness, it was a horrible thing to happen to a person. However, she'd lost her plus-one at a wedding, not the love of her life, though I supposed since Connor wasn't here to correct her, she could play any role she wanted to.

I said, "Yes, I'm really sorry." I laid her phone beside her and told her the cleaning staff had found it, and she grabbed it up.

"I've been wanting this. There are people I need to tell about Con. And I know there are pictures of us." She held the phone to her chest. I hoped she didn't start looking at her pictures while we were there, as her most recent ones were gone.

Mom, who'd already been coached, said to Tina's mom, "Why don't we go down to the coffee shop and give the girls some space?"

It seemed to me that Ruth was relieved to have an excuse to get out of this chamber of oppressive fake widowhood. She eagerly agreed, and with the ghost of a wink to me, Mom escorted her cousin Ruth out. I had no idea where Colin was, but he'd obviously made himself scarce. Now it was just the three of us, again, reminding me of our interview yesterday. And, like yesterday, I was inclined to let Jennifer continue to lead. She was proving to be surprisingly adept. Plus, of course, she didn't have the history that I had with my cousin Tina. But she'd heard all about her, so she knew that Tina could be devious and unpleasant.

Jen said, "Should we call down for some coffee?"

It turned out to be the perfect thing to say, for it gave Tina the opportunity to heave another of her great sighs and say, "I can't bear to eat or drink anything. The grief's too new. Too harsh."

Where I felt like gagging, Jennifer rose to the occasion. She put a hand over Tina's and said, "I can't imagine how you feel, but if there's anything Lucy or I can do..." She left the sentence hanging in the air. Tina really seemed to think about it as though she might have a laundry list of jobs for us, but then, to my surprise, real tears filled her eyes.

"Not unless you can bring my Con back."

I'd have thought this whole thing was a con if it wasn't for those tears. A fat drop rolled down her cheek, and she didn't even bother to wipe it away. She put the phone on the table, and I breathed a sigh of relief.

Jennifer said, "I wish I could. He was taken far too young."

"I know. That's the worst of it. We hadn't even been seeing each other that long. I mean, I felt like he was the one, you know?"

Did she? Did she really? When he was telling everybody basically that she'd been a pity date for him and hitting on all the attractive women present. If this was her idea of *the one*, I couldn't imagine what her reject pile looked like.

But Jennifer again spoke with real sympathy. I could see she'd found a place inside herself that could truly feel Tina's pain. "Why would you expect something like this to happen?"

Jennifer was doing a great job of gaining Tina's trust, mostly by showing a lot of sympathy that really seemed sincere. But also dropping leading questions. I waited for Tina to say, "He was worried that so-and-so might try to kill him," but no such luck. She only shook her head. "That's the worst. He wasn't sick or anything. One minute he was there, laughing and joking, and the next minute he was gone."

Jen reached out and touched her hand. The best thing I could do was to keep quiet and let this bonding continue. Tina wasn't a person who kept things to herself at the best of times, but under Jennifer's kindness and genuine sympathy, she really let it all hang out. How sad she was, how no one understood, how she was certain that Connor was *the one*. All the things that he wasn't around to dispute.

And, sitting back and watching, I had to admit that Tina genuinely seemed to be grieving. At first, I'd believed she was just grabbing the drama role, very much like teenage Hester, but I thought back on the way she'd wailed yesterday when she discovered Connor was dead. As theatrical as she was, her grief really did feel real.

Maybe that's why Jennifer wasn't faking her sympathy. She'd connected to the true feelings in this woman. Possibly it was partly her being a witch that made her more empathetic, but also I thought they were bonding, woman to woman.

Jennifer asked, "When did you first meet Connor?"

Oh, there couldn't have been a better question. It gave the grieving Tina a road to wallow down, and she took it. Okay, that was mean of me. However, Tina might be turning her relationship with Connor into a grand romance, but I had seen the way Connor treated her and watched him hit on other women, and I did not think there was much affection on his side.

Jennifer was smart enough, or just kind enough, to play into the idea that this had been a big romance, and when Connor's life was cut tragically short, so was Tina's future.

Tina grabbed a tissue from a nearly empty box and blew her nose. "We both grew up in Slough, and we met in school. You should have seen him. So good at wrestling. He always said he would have been a professional wrestler if there'd been enough money for proper training, but there wasn't."

"Wow, so you've been dating since school?"

She shook her head, dabbing at her eyes now. "He wasn't ready then. Too immature really. I can see that now, looking back. I won't lie to you, Jennifer. I was heartbroken when he broke things off with me. I think I knew even then that Connor was the only one for me. Still, we stayed friends."

"I can imagine how that feels." In fact, like most of us, Jennifer had had her teenage heart broken too. I felt that she was drawing on that pain to empathize with the woman in front of her. "But then you got back together again later?"

Tina nodded glumly. "I mean, we were always in each other's lives. I was the person that he always came to when he was in trouble. That's how special I was. Even if he was seeing another woman, it was me he'd turn to."

A picture was beginning to emerge and one that really did stir my pity. He'd probably come to her when he needed money or a place to crash or his washing done. I could imagine her turning herself into a doormat for Connor Townes's entitled feet, always hoping that one day he'd choose her.

All we really wanted to find out was who had asked whom to this wedding and then we could get out of here. I was finding the whole atmosphere oppressive. Which, again, I knew was very unkind of me, but I really did want to get that one piece of information out of Tina so we could get on with the investigation, hopefully solve the murder, find Rafe's painting, and then I could get on with my honeymoon.

But Jennifer worked in her own way, and I respected that. I could see that sometimes I was a bit too quick to push, but she wasn't pushing Tina for anything. She was offering a sympathetic ear and seeing what came spilling out. It wasn't the speediest way to get what she wanted, but it was obviously working. "And his job? I'm not really sure what he did for a living."

Tina's gaze dropped. She reached for the tissue box, pulling out another one even though she wasn't currently crying. After a beat of silence, she said, "Con was an entrepreneur. Had a lot of fingers in a lot of pies."

That sounded exactly like something Connor would have said about himself.

She continued, "Honestly, it was feast or famine with him.

He either had lots of money and was on top of the world, and then he spent it freely, or he'd hit tough times." She softened again. "Maybe it's wrong of me, but sometimes those were the times I liked the best. He wasn't always rushing off. He had time for me. It's not like we'd do much. He'd come round to my place and we'd sit and watch the telly. I'd cook him dinner and pour him a beer. Like a proper couple, you know?"

Again, I experienced the cringeworthy feeling that she had been the place he turned up when he had no other options. I didn't like Tina, but I was stirred by sympathy. She wasn't the first woman who'd ever been used by a man, and I doubted she'd be the last.

She held up her arm, and there was a fairly thick silver bracelet on her wrist with a curious design. She said, "He gave me that. It's a python bracelet." Now I saw that the design resembled snakeskin. "It's my most priceless possession."

Jennifer peered closer, seeming very interested. "Wow. I didn't know Connor very well, but that looks like him. I could see it on his wrist."

Tina also looked down on it and smiled. "It did use to live on his wrist. He left it at my place once, by accident really, and I started wearing it. It just made me feel close to him. At first he was annoyed when he saw me wearing it, and then he said I could keep it. It was the nicest thing he ever gave me."

Poor woman, if that was her idea of a gift.

"Did he leave other things with you?" Jennifer asked. Oh, she was good. She continued, "You know, for safekeeping? Knowing you were the person he could trust the most in the world."

Okay, I thought she was laying it on a bit thick here, but

Tina seemed to be lapping it up. "He did," she said eagerly. "He did trust me more than anyone in the world. And sometimes, yes. He would ask me to hold onto things for him. And then he'd pick them up and take them away. All part of his business, of course."

I wondered if she even realized she'd likely been concealing stolen goods. Or was I making too much of an assumption? We didn't have any concrete evidence that Connor was a thief, but the circumstantial evidence suggested it was likely. And if he'd leave a stolen item with her once, mightn't he do it again?

I spoke up now. "Did he give you anything to look after during my wedding?" *Like a priceless painting?*

"No. Why would he?" Then she got all teary. "Look, I really—"

Jennifer said quickly, "I'm so glad I got a chance to meet Connor." Then she laughed. "It's always funny at weddings, isn't it? To see everyone all dressed up. But you two looked good together."

The little they'd actually been together.

Tina brightened and leaned toward Jen like a flower to the sun. "I know."

"Did you have any trouble convincing him to come?" Jen asked. "Lots of men hate getting dragged to weddings. I couldn't even find a date."

Tina nodded. "I know what you mean. Took a bit of persuading until I told him where the wedding was. He reckoned it would be nice to see inside such a grand house."

And there it was, the answer we'd been looking for. She had definitely asked Connor to be her date to my wedding. It even sounded like he'd been going to say no until he'd discovered the venue.

"I guess Connor's family will be devastated," Jennifer said.

Tina shook her head, and her face went hard. "He doesn't have any family. His dad left when he was little, and he doesn't speak to his mom. I'm his family, really."

"Wow. No brothers or sisters?"

Tina shook her head again. "He was an only child. He always said his parents let him know he was a mistake."

Ouch. I hadn't liked Connor very much, but I couldn't imagine growing up always feeling you were unwanted. Maybe that was why he kept gravitating back to Tina. She wasn't the woman of his dreams, but she so clearly wanted him and would do anything to prove it.

Tina then rubbed her hand across her eyes. "I don't even want to leave Oxford now. I feel like he's still here, you know? It just won't be the same when I go home to Sidmouth and he doesn't drop round to borrow my car or borrow a few quid 'cause he's short."

She was not painting the view of a grand love affair that she thought she was. Like Jennifer, my sympathy was becoming real.

Jennifer sent me a quick glance, but I thought she'd done a fabulous job and found out everything that there was to find out. I gave her the tiniest of nods, and she said, "I'm just so sorry again. We won't take up any more of your time."

Tina nodded and almost looked sorry we were leaving. "I've got to get packed up anyway. We have to check out today." And then she sent me a resentful look as though putting her and her parents up for a whole weekend wasn't enough. Mind you, I couldn't have known that her date would end up dead.

I said, "I'm really sorry too."

And then, realizing that I had a lot more resources at my disposal than I used to, I said, "I'm sure if you want to stay another day or two, it would be all right. I can ask Rafe."

The old Tina came out in a sudden sneer. "Not a very good start to your marriage, is it? If you have to ask permission from your husband."

I let it go. She'd been flinging barbs at me since we first met, so I just stood up and said, "Let the front desk know if you want to stay on. I'll arrange it with Rafe."

Jennifer said the rest of our goodbyes, and then we found ourselves back outside in the hall. Neither of us said a word until we were standing in front of the elevator out of earshot.

Jennifer let out a loud breath and said, "Phew."

I couldn't help it. I said, "You were amazing in there. You should join MI5."

She seemed quite flattered by my comment. "Really? I was honestly just going with my instinct. And hers. I could pick up her genuine grief."

I nodded. "Me too. I think she cared about Connor a lot more than we realized."

"A lot more than he deserved."

"And we found out that she definitely invited him to the wedding, so we can tick that item off our list," I said, feeling virtuous.

Jen said, "We found out more than that. It's like she was obsessed with him."

"Which turned her into a doormat."

"Have you ever felt that way about a man?" she asked.

Was this a loaded question? "Do you think I'm obsessed with Rafe?"

She laughed in surprise. "No. Not at all. Your love is the kind we all want, even if it does come with some issues. But not everybody gets so lucky. Maybe Tina didn't know the difference between someone who loves you and someone who just uses you."

"I feel there's a lot about Connor Townes that we don't know, but the picture we're getting of his character isn't anything you'd want to say in his eulogy."

She looked at me, and her eyes opened wide. "Speaking of eulogies, do we have to go to his funeral?"

My eyes must have mirrored hers. "I don't know. Maybe if we can figure out how he died, we won't have to."

"Good plan."

CHAPTER 12

We hit the lobby just as the mothers were embracing, having clearly finished their coffee. I said my goodbyes to Tina's mother, and then my mom, Jennifer, and I headed back out into the sunshine. I had initially just thought bringing my mother along was a good way to separate Tina from Ruth, but what I hadn't taken into account was that young women weren't the only ones who liked to share with their female friends.

Mom was practically bursting with news as we walked back to the car. She said, "Well, I won't say Ruth is happy that Connor Townes is dead, but she is clearly relieved that her daughter will no longer be enthralled by that man."

I turned to her. "Enthralled? Did she actually use that word?"

"She did. She said he had an unnatural hold over her daughter. All he had to do was snap his fingers, and she'd do anything for him. The money she's lent him, which she never got back; the times she's dropped everything to go and pick him up because he needed her. And he used to borrow her car and run it completely out of petrol, return it filthy. She never said a word. Not one complaint. Doormat, that's what she was. Nothing but a doormat, poor girl."

That was pretty much what we'd discovered too. Jennifer said, "But why would Connor need Tina's car when he had his own? And he was so proud of it." She did a pretty bad imitation of Connor Townes's voice, "Got a Jensen Interceptor, haven't I? Very rare. She's my pride and joy, she is."

I said, "I'm not positive, but is it possible that because his car was quite recognizable he preferred a more nondescript vehicle, which I'm guessing is what Tina has?"

My mother nodded, pleased to have information we didn't. "It is. A Ford Mondeo."

I turned to her. "A Ford Mondeo?" That was a classic family car. The kind of car my dad would drive.

Mom nodded. "It was their family car, and when they got a new one, they gave the old one to Tina. So I think it annoyed her even more that he would borrow what she basically considered to be their family car and treat it so poorly."

"They don't get more forgettable than that. I don't suppose she mentioned the color?"

"No, but I'll bet you pounds to pennies it was gray. Or blue. They aren't the kind of people to pick a daring color."

"So it would be perfect for the kind of jobs where you want to slip in and slip out unseen."

Mom glanced at me sharply. "You think he was involved in criminal activities?"

"The police sure knew who he was. And he definitely seemed untrustworthy." We had decided not to tell my parents about the missing painting, certainly not before Rafe and my dad had their evening out.

Mom nodded. "That's exactly what my cousin believes. She was convinced he was using Tina and, by extension, them as a respectable front for crime."

"Didn't Ruth and Colin retire to Dorset and Tina moved down to be near them?"

"Devon actually," Mom said. "You'll have the addresses somewhere for the thank-you cards."

Oh, right. There were the thank-you cards to send out, and that was another ceremonial nightmare. What kind of card did you send someone who brought a date and then he got killed? Thanks for the lovely coffee maker, sorry about your dead date?

I'd figure that out later. The vampires had been around forever. They probably had some idea of the etiquette around this. Maybe we'd send some flowers. Flowers were always good after a death.

There was no way Connor could have left the wedding, driven to Tina's place, where I would bet my knitting shop he had a key, stashed the painting and driven back before anyone noticed.

But could he have passed the portrait to Tina? I said aloud, "Do you think Tina could have been an actual accomplice?" I turned to Mom. "What do you think?"

She moved her mouth as though she was actually chewing on it and then said, "I don't think she would play an active role in Connor's criminal activity."

Oddly, even though I didn't like Tina, that opinion tallied with mine. I didn't think so either.

"Besides," Jennifer said, "as I said before, he offered to take me out on the river after your wedding. I agreed to look at his car but that was all I was interested in."

So it didn't seem like he'd planned a mad dash to Devon.

We dropped Mom off, and then I asked Jen if she minded coming with me to see Margaret Twigg. "Maybe you'd rather do some sightseeing in Oxford." I felt like she'd barely seen anything. "There are walking tours of the city, or you can tour some of the colleges—"

"I can sightsee anytime. I'm coming with you to visit the Wicked Witch of Wychwood," she said.

Great. If I had to visit Margaret Twigg, I wanted the company. "At least it's a pretty drive." Margaret Twigg lived in an old stone cottage set in what remained of the once-large forest of Wychwood. As we drove, I pointed out the hidden site, not too far off the road, where an ancient circle of standing stones was often the site of our coven ceremonies. Then the road dipped, and we entered what was left of the forest. Margaret's cottage sat alone and forbidding. Made of ancient stone, tucked in the shade of the trees, it looked exactly like the kind of place you'd expect to find a witch.

We parked and walked up to her door. "Ready?" I asked Jen.

"Let's do this." And she knocked on the thick oak door.

Margaret Twigg didn't seem a lot more excited to see me than I was to see her.

She led us into her kitchen, where something that smelled faintly of licorice was brewing in her cauldron over the fire. She stirred the potion and over her shoulder asked, "What is it you want?"

No pleasantries, no offer of tea or coffee. She was a busy witch with no time to waste. I was perfectly happy to be in and out of her presence as soon as possible.

Jen was taking in the surroundings. The modern kitchen

mixed with the old. Tools of witchcraft alongside a modern toaster and high-end electric mixer.

I asked Margaret if she'd ever heard of a river spirit in the Cherwell.

She smiled sourly. "Did you think we were the only magical creatures? Naturally there are water gods."

Obviously, I was acquainted with vampires. I was nearly killed by a demon. Ghosts didn't bother me until they got unruly. But still. Water gods?

"You mean like Poseidon?" Jen asked. She'd obviously paid more attention in school than I had.

"Or Neptune?" I added, not to be outdone.

Margaret gave me that look that I swore she'd perfected for me. "They are virtually the same, Lucy. Poseidon is the Greek god of the sea, and Neptune is the Roman equivalent. Obviously, you won't find either of them in the Cherwell River, but there's a Celtic water spirit who lives there. Morgen."

So the rumors Carlos had heard were true. "Is there a spell we can use to get this creature to appear?"

"You don't summon Morgen with a spell. You ask nicely." She thought for a minute. "And it's always good to have something to offer."

I was horrified. "You mean like a blood sacrifice?"

Margaret Twigg shook her head so her Medusa curls shook. "I mean like a hospitality gift."

"What do you give the river god who has everything?" I sounded sarcastic. I felt sarcastic.

"A towel?" Jennifer offered.

I snorted with laughter. "Bathing cap?"

"Maybe a nice shower gel?"

We were cracking each other up. Margaret Twigg was not amused, which made us giggle harder. Finally, she said, "You may take this schoolgirl nonsense elsewhere," and snapped her fingers, and we found ourselves outside her cottage. As I turned in shock, impressed and awed as usual by her powers, the open door slammed in our faces.

We were on our own.

∼

"Now what?" Jen asked. Neither of us suggested knocking on the door and trying to get back into the cottage.

"At least we know there's a river spirit. And we have its name."

I had no idea where we were going to find the right offering for this river spirit. Jen wasn't much help. "Do we give it something to eat?"

With Margaret Twigg having slammed the door in our faces, I decided to ask Rafe. He'd lived in Oxford on and off for a long while. Perhaps he knew what to offer a river spirit.

There was no one better to ask about stuff like this than Rafe. We got back into my car and drove to the manor house. We found Rafe in his office studying an illuminated manuscript.

"Wow," I said, looking over his shoulder. "That's beautiful."

"Yes," he said. "Also a fake."

That's why colleges and libraries consulted him. He saved them a lot of money by weeding out the fakes from the real thing.

He glanced up at me and Jen and looked rather amused.

"Whenever you two are together looking at me in that way, I know you're going to ask me to do something I don't want to do."

I tried to look offended, but it was hard when he was so right. "You're my husband. Aren't you supposed to do unpleasant things that I want you to do?"

"I don't think you're going to ask me to take out the recycling, are you?"

He had me there. Besides, when had Rafe ever taken out the recycling? He had staff for that.

Briefly, I explained about the river deity and the need for an offering. "But we have no idea what to offer." I spared him our discussion on shower gels.

"Most deities I've come across are quite mercenary. What do we know about this spirit?" he asked. The nice thing about Rafe, and I suppose any supernatural creature, is you skip right past the "What? There's a spirit in the river!" conversation. He might have even known about it. He knew a lot of things.

"Margaret Twigg said his name is Morgen."

"Ah, likely an offspring of the Sea-Morgen," he said. "A fisherman and a sea creature got together and had children. Morgen is likely one of them. I'd try a coin."

"But I don't know what kind of coin to chuck in the river to encourage a water spirit to have a conversation," I said. "A pound coin doesn't seem very special. If it were that easy, everyone who tossed a coin in water to make a wish could summon a spirit."

Rafe stood up and turned to us. "Let's have a look at my collection. I imagine I've got something that would tempt this Morgen." He thought for a minute. "My suggestion is to keep it in the family." And then he beckoned the two of us to follow him.

Rafe's manor house was quite large. And while I'd spent time in all the main rooms, there were bits I still had never seen. He took us along a corridor and around a bend into the other wing. The one that no one much went into. I'd mostly assumed it was just storage and unused rooms down this way, but it was more like a library or museum. This was where Rafe kept things. I wasn't going to say the man was a hoarder, but he'd been alive so long he had a lot of belongings that were presumably sentimental to him or just important enough that he felt they should be preserved. Like that missing painting.

I could see that Lochlan and his team had been busy down here too. The security system was clearly up and running. I knew it irked Rafe, but he didn't say anything. He led us into a room that was more like a gallery. There were a few lesser paintings on the walls and then pull-out drawers that had obviously been specially built for the space. They were beautiful. Made of special inlaid wood, walnut, I thought.

He said, "There was a time when I collected coins. I still pick up the occasional thing that interests me."

I could see now that the drawers were all neatly labeled. It didn't take him any time at all to reach for one and pull it out.

I said, "Wow." It looked like a drawer out of a museum. And probably could have been. I went closer to peek, and there were coins so old you could barely make out what was on them.

He said, "This is my Greek section." He pulled out a magnifying glass and started scanning across them. We stood silently back. I looked over at Jen, and if her face reflected mine, it was pretty amazed.

Then he nodded. "I thought I had one of these." He reached in and picked up a coin. He said, "I'll polish it up for you. The silver's gone dull, but that's the head of Poseidon." He passed it to me, and Jen and I both peered at the silver disk. "It's from 227 BC."

"It's so well-preserved," Jen said. It was, too. The head of Poseidon was in profile. He looked very serious, with a strong nose, deep-set eyes and a full head of curly hair and a beard. Something that looked like a cross between a crown and a hairband wrapped around his head.

I wasn't sure about this. "Won't Morgen want gold?"

"I think he'll be pretty pleased with this. It's quite rare."

Jen said, "Is it worth a lot of money?"

He said, "I don't really keep up with current values, but I wouldn't think it's worth more than about ten thousand."

I said, "Ten thousand pounds?"

He shrugged. "Somewhere around there, I think."

"I can't take a coin that valuable and throw it in the river."

"Lucy, I have an enormous collection. This isn't one of the more valuable ones. And besides, I'd happily spend ten thousand pounds if it could hurry us up on our honeymoon."

Well, in that case.

I said, "Okay. And if it doesn't summon this creature, will you be mad at me?"

"Not at all. Someday, some diver will get a nice surprise."

I tossed the coin in the air and caught it. "When shall we pay a visit to this Morgen?" I asked Jen.

"Tonight," she said. "Because I'll be heading to Cornwall

soon and I don't want to miss my chance to summon a river spirit. We'll go tonight when it's quiet."

"Makes sense."

"I'm going with you," Rafe said. Before I could argue, he said, "I'll stay out of the way, but I need to be close in case anything happens."

Jen, probably guessing I might try to argue with Rafe and that it would be futile, said, "Let's get back to the knitting shop. I have a feeling I'd better start packing."

It seemed wrong that her holiday was being derailed by investigating suspicious deaths and hanging around with the undead. "Are you sure you don't mind going to Cornwall with Sylvia and my grandmother?"

She shook her head. "Honestly, I'm looking forward to it. I've never been to Cornwall before, and I hear it's beautiful. There's so many movies and TV shows that have been made there, and I always loved the Daphne du Maurier novels."

We heaved an identical sigh and said in unison, *"Rebecca."* We'd both read it in high school and fallen in love with Max de Winter. Rebecca was a classic Cinderella story and we'd both imagined being swept away by a romantic older man who was both wealthy and enigmatic. Weirdly, I'd kind of lived that story.

I dropped Jennifer back at the flat, and before she got out of the car, my mother phoned and said, "Your father has invited Simon Pattengale and his wife to have dinner with us tonight. I'm terribly annoyed with him because I was hoping we could have dinner with you and Rafe. In all the busyness of the wedding and now this dreadful death, I feel like we haven't had much time together, as a family."

I could have kissed her. What a perfect opening. I knew

that Rafe had intended to get together with my dad and the doctor over brandies, but this was so much more perfect. An event arranged by my parents. We could have dinner, and then it would be the most natural thing in the world for Rafe to suggest brandy with the two older men while my mom and I went for a walk or something. Rafe didn't love having dinner in restaurants for obvious reasons, but he could manage with a steak tartare or a very rare steak. And I was getting pretty good at sharing food off his plate. Honestly, sometimes it was like I ate two meals.

I said that was perfect, and we agreed to meet in Oxford for dinner that evening. I asked Jen if she wanted to join us, but she said, "No offense, Luce, but an evening with your parents and their friends is kind of dull. Pete and Meri said they'd take me to a dinner party with some grad students. Plus, I really need to do some washing and pack."

I was delighted she had something to do with people our age so I could enjoy my much older man, and even if the dinner was dull, it would hopefully lead to a clue or at least we'd cross out one avenue of inquiry.

"We should be finished dinner by nine. Shall we meet up then to try to talk to Morgen? Or do you want to stay at your dinner party? I could go alone," I said, sounding not at all brave.

"No. I'm coming. I'll meet you here at nine."

"Perfect." Feeling incredibly pleased at how smoothly this investigation was falling into place, I drove back to the manor house. Lochlan was there, and he and Rafe were walking around, obviously discussing the security system. I felt so bad. Rafe had never needed one before. I knew I had brought a lot of good things into his life, but I was a little worried that I'd brought some not-so-good things along with me as well.

They both seemed pleased to see me, and Lochlan wanted to know what we'd found out.

I caught him up and told both of them the gist of the conversation we'd had with Tina.

Lochlan said, "So she definitely invited him."

"Yes," I confirmed. "She definitely did.

"However," I said, because I had been thinking about this, "if he's been hanging around with thieves and low-lifes, he's exactly the kind of guy who would brag about a wedding invitation to a place like this." Here I waved my hand around the luxurious surroundings. "And word could easily have gotten back to someone who knew or suspected there were treasures here. So I'm not entirely sure that it was just a crime of opportunity."

"And yet so few people know about the double-sided gallery," Lochlan said. "Why not grab a painting off the wall, like that Botticelli," he said, pointing. It was a small painting of the Madonna with a sweet smile. "Or a piece of Georgian silver, or he could have gone looking for jewelry or cash. Even one of your priceless books would have been small enough to hide under his jacket."

"Maybe he was snooping in the gallery room and stumbled on it somehow?" It's not like they were locked, more like if you didn't know the panels opened, how would you figure it out?

We stood there, and none of us had any new ideas to put forward. I had a bit of good news, though in the scheme of things, it was pretty insignificant. "I know you were looking for an opportunity to talk to Dr. Pattengale, and I'm happy to report that my parents have invited us for dinner along with the doctor and his wife tonight."

"Well, that's convenient," Lochlan said. "And while you're out, I'll be able to get on with installing more of the security system."

To me, he said, with an edge to his voice, "And keep your husband away from here as long as you can."

I had to stifle a grin. I could imagine that Rafe was not the easiest customer, especially as he didn't even want a security system. However, like Lochlan, I appreciated that he needed one.

Not wishing to get in between these two, I said, "We're meeting at seven at that new French restaurant my dad's been wanting to try. I hope that's okay."

"Of course. I didn't have anything on my calendar for today anyway." Ouch. Because we should have been on our honeymoon at this point, not still hanging around Oxford trying to find missing paintings and solve murders. And I was pretty sure dinner with my parents and a possible suspect wasn't exactly what he'd had planned for this evening.

I went over and slipped my hand into his. "We will get on our honeymoon, I promise."

He smiled down at me. "I know."

"And after dinner, we'll go to the river and see if we can summon Morgen."

I SPENT the afternoon with Olivia cleaning out one of the stone outbuildings so I could have it for my craft. I chose one that was near the walled garden. I liked the energy in this part of the estate and thought of Artemis keeping an eye on things when I was away. Everything on the estate was well maintained, so it was only a question of sweeping it out, washing the small windows, and bringing in a few cabinets. The old fireplace worked, she said, but the chimney should be cleaned before I used it.

This was fine, as I had no intention of brewing potions on hot summer days. I'd wait until the fall. However, there was a lovely thick oak beam running through the center of the roof that would be perfect for hanging herbs, and when we'd hauled in a couple of old oak cabinets, the small cottage began to feel like mine. Naturally, Nyx came in to see what was up. She sniffed all around the stone floor and stuck her nose in all the corners. I wouldn't have to worry about mice. I cleansed the space with burning sage and then put a protection spell around the perimeter. Lochlan had his security system, and I had mine.

I moved the crystal ball from the room where I'd been storing it and placed it carefully on an alcove, then I placed the tools of my craft in the drawers and cupboards.

I put my broom in the corner, and Nyx immediately went over to it and looked back at me.

"No ride tonight, I'm afraid," I told her. "I have a dinner date."

She sniffed at that and walked out.

AFTER SHOWERING off the dust of a busy afternoon, I changed into a blue linen dress and matched it with a lacy cream-colored cardigan made of alpaca and silk that Theodore had knit for me. Sylvia had been encouraging, no, nagging me to start shopping at more expensive places now that I was with Rafe, but I liked my simple wardrobe just fine, and when I'd asked him, he told me he liked it too. I was about to put on the diamond necklace Sylvia had given me when my new husband came up behind me, kissed the back of my neck and said, "Try this one."

He slipped a necklace around my neck and fastened it before letting me run to the mirror and look. "It's perfect," I said, staring at the dazzling piece in the mirror. it was a delicate princess necklace of diamonds and sapphires that was beautiful without being overwhelming.

"I love it," I said, turning this way and that.

"It suits you," he said, sounding pleased. "I've got a collection of jewels I've picked up over the years, but I bought this one new for you. I saw it and knew it would look right."

I ran up and threw my arms around him. "You are the best husband ever," I said.

He looked down at me with a wry smile. "Let's see if you still feel that way when we've been married an entire week." Then he kissed me. "There are earrings to match," he said, handing me a blue box.

"You got this at Tiffany's?" I cried. That seemed so fancy.

"I did. And when we have time, you must look over the collection and see what you want remounted. Most of the jewels are too heavy for you. Too ostentatious."

"Yes," I said airily, striking a pose like something Sylvia might do, "ostentatious is so last century."

When I'd finished dressing, Rafe and I headed off to meet my parents. It was nearly impossible for Rafe to go out in Oxford without knowing someone. He not only had a reputation for evaluating and restoring old manuscripts in a city where there were an awful lot of them, but he still occasionally gave lectures at Cardinal College, just down the street from my wool shop. He was also on several boards and a generous donor to local charities. He also was incredibly good-looking, still appeared to be thirty-five years old, and was quietly wealthy. I really don't think I'm boasting when I say there were some pretty chagrined women in Oxford now that he had married me.

We walked into the restaurant, and several people hailed him, including the president of Cardinal College. Then a hand went up, and we saw my parents sitting at a round table in a quiet corner, Simon Pattengale and his wife, Prunella, with them.

I wasn't sure how this evening would go since neither of us knew the doctor or his wife very well. He and my dad went way back. I hoped it wouldn't be the four of them reminiscing about their old days at Oxford while Rafe pretended to eat and I stuffed myself on two dinners instead of one.

However, when we got there, Mrs. Pattengale told me again how much she'd enjoyed the wedding, and then we had to talk about that while we perused the menu. Then my sharp-eyed mother asked about the necklace and earrings, and when everyone had admired the set, the talk immediately turned to the tragedy of Connor Townes dying. Dr. Pattengale seemed quite stunned.

"I don't even practice medicine anymore, and here I've been called on twice in the space of forty-eight hours."

"And not exactly what I'd imagined when I pictured my wedding festivities," I said.

My mom immediately patted my hand. "You couldn't

have known, dear. I blame myself for inviting Tina. I've always felt rather sorry for that girl, but I can see it was a mistake. I couldn't be more sorry."

My dad said, "Nonsense. None of us could have known what would happen. And Rafe and Lucy's wedding was perfect. The unpleasantness was at the event we organized."

That was nice of him to say so. The doctor said, "And wasn't it lucky that young man who fell out of the window wasn't badly hurt." He turned to Rafe. "How is he, by the way?"

Rafe was able to tell him, with complete truth, that Guy had suffered no lasting injuries. In fact, he hadn't suffered any injuries at all, being a vampire.

I thought he'd been more stunned than anything.

I chose a sole meunière, a deliberately light meal, knowing I'd be eating for two, and Rafe settled on lamb done with a mustard and wine sauce that sounded delicious. Mom dithered as she always did in restaurants and finally settled on moules et frites, mussels and fries. Mrs. Pattengale had salmon poached in licorice, and both my dad and Dr. Pattengale went for steaks. Dad chose a red and a white wine, and then we settled back to enjoy the evening. Or not.

I felt a little nervous in my stomach. I think it was knowing that Rafe was going to try to get my dad and the doctor separated from us so that he could do his bit of sleuthing, but weirdly, my dad made that unnecessary. I had never thought of my dad as a blabbermouth, but I began to realize that he'd been working in the desert so long, he'd lost that sense of discretion that instinctively tells you when something is meant to be kept secret and when it's okay to share it. Or maybe he'd never had that skill, I don't know. As we sipped wine and nibbled on a couple of appetizer sharing plates, he couldn't stop talking about how beautiful the wedding was and what a lovely bride I'd made.

He turned to the doctor. "Our whole lives, we imagined this day." Then he turned to my mom. "Well, more Susan than I. We only have the one child, you see, and we always hoped she'd marry someone nice."

My mom nodded, looking pleased.

My dad, who should have stopped there, chuckled and said, "You should have seen the one she dated before Rafe. Todd, his name was. We tried to like him, for her sake, but he really wasn't worthy—"

"Anyway," my mom said in a loud voice, "that's ancient history." I could tell from the way my dad suddenly jumped that she'd stepped on his foot with her heel or kicked him in the ankle.

If it wasn't so embarrassing, it would have been funny.

The doctor's wife said, "Oh, I know. You can see the bad ones a mile away, but they don't listen to us."

I thought about how Tina's mother had been moaning away to my mom about Connor and supposed it was true. No doubt my parents had tried to steer me away from Todd, but I'd wasted two years of my life on him. Still, it had all worked out in the end. If he hadn't broken my heart, I wouldn't have moved to Oxford, and then I never would have met Rafe. I glanced up at him. And that had turned out pretty well. So far.

As though they were all thinking the same thing, my mom said, "We couldn't be happier with the man our Lucy has chosen."

Rafe took the compliment with grace and said, "And I'll do everything I can to make Lucy happy."

"I'll try to make you happy, too," I said.

"You already do."

Our food arrived, and Dad ordered more wine. I thought he and his old school friend were having a contest to see who could drink the most. Like they were back in college.

The talk turned to an art exhibition of old masters at the National Gallery in London that the Pattengales had been to see and encouraged my parents to visit before they left. Then the doctor, who was putting away the wine pretty freely, suddenly said, "Of course, you could simply go to your son-in-law's home. Imagine owning a Rembrandt."

There was the sound of metal hitting china as my fork dropped out of my hand and hit my plate. The only Rembrandt Rafe had was hidden behind the panels in his private art collection. Rafe looked at me, and I said, assuming this was what he wanted, "How did you know Rafe had a Rembrandt?" all innocent-like.

Dr. Pattengale looked confused. "Is it a secret?" Then he looked at my dad. "Jack told me."

My dad shook his head. "I don't think so. I'm sure I mentioned Rafe's art gallery. It's the most remarkable thing. You turn the panels, and one set of paintings on a wall turns into a completely different set." My dad was partaking freely of the wine too at this point. "But have you got a Rembrandt? You didn't show it to me."

Rafe was looking very keenly at Simon Pattengale now. "It was out for cleaning when I showed you my collection. The Rembrandt only came back a few days ago."

There was a terrible silence. The doctor glanced at his

wife as though she might save him from social embarrassment, but she was staring at him with as much shock as the rest of us were.

Finally, he said, going very red in the face, "Oh dear. This is rather awkward. I didn't think anyone would mind. I went into the gallery and opened the panels. It's very clever the way the brass knobs turn to reveal a second collection. To have such a wealth of art to oneself, even for a few moments, was incredible." He turned to Rafe. "I'm sorry if I did wrong. I definitely should have asked you first. I was simply overwhelmed with the idea that these beautiful paintings were right there. Art is my passion."

Rafe said, "Well, I would have been happy to show you if you'd asked."

He said it pleasantly enough, but there was an edge of steel to his words.

My dad looked distinctly uncomfortable. "Should I not have said anything?" He was looking at my mom.

She said, "We'll talk about this later."

I felt both my plate of food and Rafe's plate of food get stuck somewhere between my mouth and my stomach. I hated social awkwardness, and there was a big, huge cloud of it floating around our table right now.

The doctor said, "Honestly, I'm most dreadfully sorry. I don't know what came over me. I may have had a glass of champagne too many. But it really is a most remarkable collection."

"I very much hope you'll keep what you saw to yourself," Rafe said. "I'm a very private man, and that's a very private collection."

"Oh, yes, absolutely. And one wouldn't want word to get

out. There are thieves who would pay a fortune for master-pieces like that."

"Exactly," Rafe said dryly.

And then my dad, who clearly realized he'd screwed up in some way but was still slightly foggy about how, said, "Anyway, Susan and I will definitely book a day out in London to see that exhibit. And wasn't there something at the Tate you were keen on, my love?"

The rest of the evening passed pleasantly enough, although there was a touch of awkwardness about the whole evening. I was wondering if the doctor had done more than just look at the treasures in Rafe's collection. Had he helped himself to something small and valuable? I was certain Rafe was thinking the same thing. And what did we do now? It was one thing to break into Connor Townes's flat, knowing he was dead, but were we really going to snoop through the home of a friend of my father's? Hoping to find a stolen painting?

But what if he had taken it?

At least, since we'd had the whole conversation over dinner, Rafe wasn't obliged to take the men for brandies. Instead, the doctor and his wife invited us all back to their place for an after-dinner drink. I wondered whether Rafe would want to go so that he could do some snooping, though I wondered how he'd pull that off. It wasn't like you could say, "Can I please use the bathroom" and then search the place.

I glanced at him, and he said, "If you don't mind, we'll take a raincheck."

I was so glad he'd read my expression correctly. I did not want to spend any more of the evening with my parents and their friends, especially now that we knew the doctor had taken himself on a private tour of Rafe's house. Our house now, as I kept having to remind myself.

I'd been very careful not to drink much wine, as I still had river spirits to summon. As we settled into the car for the short drive to pick up Jennifer, I said, "What do you think?"

"That's an open-ended question. What do I think about what?"

He was in a surprisingly good mood for a guy who was missing a very valuable painting and who'd just discovered that one of my father's friends had acted inappropriately during our wedding ceremony.

"I mean, what do you think about the doctor? Did he take the portrait of Elizabeth?"

"It's possible."

"You don't seem very upset."

"I'm pleased. It's a solid lead."

I turned to stare at him. "So you are planning to investigate his house?"

"No question. I don't even feel guilty. He certainly made free use of our house. I'll return the favor and look in all the nooks and crannies of his private space."

I had to admit there was a kind of justice on his side.

"What will you do if you find it?"

When he smiled, his teeth were very white. "I will return it to its rightful place. And make certain that in future nothing gets past Lochlan's security system. He claims it's the best in the world."

"We could have that painting back very soon, then," I said. I felt so relieved but also horrified. "Shouldn't Dr. Pattengale go to jail for stealing a painting that valuable?"

"Probably. But when he finds it's missing, he'll make an

educated guess that I have reclaimed my property, and then he'll spend the rest of his life wondering whether I'll turn him in." He chuckled. "I think that might be punishment enough."

I wasn't so certain but didn't want to spoil Rafe's good mood. I only hoped the portrait was easy to find. "When are you going to search his home?"

"I'll get Lochlan's staff to put surveillance on the house. As soon as it's empty, we'll slip in and do a thorough search. He'll never know we were there. Unless he discovers he's missing a stolen painting."

"Unless Morgen the river spirit knows where to find it."

His phone buzzed, and he looked at it. "Lochlan's called a knitting club meeting tonight."

"But I don't know how long it will take Jen and me to find this Morgen. Assuming he even shows."

"No one is in a hurry. The meeting won't start until we get there."

"Right. They'll just get more knitting done."

CHAPTER 13

*W*e picked Jen up, and then Rafe drove us toward the Cherwell River. "Do people punt at night?" I asked Rafe.

"The punt rental companies want their punts back by sunset," he said, "but some people do punt at night."

"Let's see if the place where Connor supposedly rented boats from will rent us a punt," I said.

"But weren't those guys gone when the police went to look for them?" Jen said.

"I don't know. I have a feeling. The great-aunt still lives there, so maybe she can tell us something or let us borrow a boat." I was reaching, I knew, but I felt that I needed to see the place where Connor's supposed friends had operated from. Jason Smith had disappeared but I wondered if there'd be a clue he'd left behind.

Jen completely understood that a witch's instinct was worth following, so we agreed. Rafe drove us to the house, which was exactly as my mom had described it. A big, kind of creepy-looking Victorian with a weeping willow in the front yard. The place looked a bit unkempt, but there was a light on inside. I suggested we go around the back where the punts would be.

Rafe would have come with us, but I asked him not to. I felt that we witches needed to do this next part on our own. "If we don't get a punt, we'll walk down to the river and try to call the spirit," I explained.

He wasn't happy, but he must have understood that he'd be a hindrance rather than a help. "I'll stay close," he promised. "All you have to do is call me."

"I know." It was comforting knowing we had backup.

Jen and I skirted the big old house, finding a path down the side that sloped downhill in the direction of the river. It was quiet, and I jumped when something rustled in the trees. A mouse probably. Or a rat.

Behind the big house was a fenced area. Some of the fencing was clearly new. As we approached in the dim light, I made out the figure of a man standing on the other side of the fence. A gate was open, so we walked through it. This was definitely the boatyard. There were half a dozen punts lined up. "Hi," I said.

He turned. He was probably close to our age, wearing jeans and a windbreaker. "Help you?" he asked, sounding like helping us was the last thing he wanted to do.

Could this be one of the thieves and fences? He didn't seem the type, but then, as I'd discovered with criminals, sometimes you really couldn't tell.

"We wanted to rent a punt," I said, as though it was perfectly normal to show up at nine-fifteen on a Monday night and take a trip on the river.

"I don't know. I'm looking for the owner myself. Owes me

money, he does. I've been working here, but they don't seem to be open."

Jen spoke up, "We're from America. We were really hoping to take a punt out tonight. We'll pay cash."

He seemed to ponder the offer, then nodded. "Why not? A hundred quid for the two of you."

I suspected a hundred pounds was above the going rate, but we weren't about to quibble.

"Thanks," said Jen, pulling out her wallet. Luckily, she had cash on her and quickly counted out five twenties. Before she handed it into his open palm, she said, "But you'll have to help us carry the boat down to the water."

"No problem," he said, cheering up now that he had some cash coming his way.

The three of us hefted the boat up, and the man we'd rented the punt from carried the long wooden punting pole. It wasn't far to the water's edge, and I wanted to get as much info from him as I could. I said, "Do you know the owners?"

"Not really. I answered an ad for casual work. The owners are a couple of wide boys. One of them has an aunt who owns the house."

I was confused. "Wide boys?" I wondered if they were hefty men. As in large in girth.

He nodded, seeing my confused face, added, "You know, spivs."

I was more confused by the second. "Spivs?"

"Yeah. Not chavs, better dressed than that. Think they're a bit of class, but they aren't."

I had to admit, "I have no idea what you're talking about. Could you describe these people?"

He scratched his head. "You know, wide boys. Think they're a better class of criminal. They wear proper shirts, pair of nice trousers, maybe a jacket. Shine their shoes, don't they. Swagger around, always got a deal on the go, but deep down they're just a bunch of thieves and con men."

Ah. Maybe I didn't have the vocabulary, but I knew exactly what he meant. I said, "So, you didn't feel this was a legitimate operation."

"I think they hoped to fleece tourists using the old aunt's premises." Since I was pretty sure he'd just fleeced us, I imagined he knew.

"Did you know Connor Townes?" I asked.

We'd reached the river, and the three of us put the punt down on the soft ground of the river bank. It was shallow here, and I could see it would only need a push to put the boat in the water.

He said, "Yeah, I think so. He was friends with the two who ran the punting operation. They were a sight, the three of them. He died, you know. Connor Townes. Out on the river, I heard." He didn't sound too broken up about it.

"Was Connor Townes a wide boy?" I asked.

He made a noise with his tongue clicking the roof of his mouth, pointed at me. "Now you're catching on."

I could see we were going to lose him soon. What other information could I glean? "Were they making money at this?"

He shrugged. "Maybe. They weren't paying me much, I can tell you that. But it was weird. The boats were always coming back with weeds all over the bottom, so I'd have to scrape them all off or there'll be a crack in the hull, or I go to

155

get the poles and they'd be missing. I asked a fellow who worked for one of the other companies, and he said they never had that problem. You ask me, either that old house is haunted or these boats are possessed."

Then he handed me the punting pole. "Right. Off you go. Have fun." Then he looked around vaguely. We could see the lights of one of the colleges on the other side of the river, but mostly it was gloomy where we stood. "Bring it back here when you're finished," he said. I didn't imagine he'd be here to collect the boat, but it wasn't really our affair.

He helped us put the boat into the water and even held it steady as we climbed in, stepping into the middle of the boat so as not to rock it too much. We both sat on bare wooden seats. In the photos I'd seen of punting there were cushions, but I didn't imagine any were going to be forthcoming.

I could see he wanted to be on his way, but some instinct of chivalry made him say, "Stand on the back of the boat, there, and let the punting pole slide down until it hits the bottom. Then push off. You'll get the hang of it. When you've gone as far as you want to, turn around and come back here."

"Right," Jen said, sounding more confident than I felt. "Shouldn't be too difficult." She took the pole from him and moved to the back. She pushed off, and I grabbed a low-hanging branch to stop us going into the bushes. I pushed away, and behind us I heard the young guy say, "Cheerio."

She pushed us forward again and managed to get us closer to the middle of the river, which wasn't very wide. I only hoped it was as shallow as everyone said, just in case.

"Are we sure we want to do this?" I asked Jen as we looked over the quiet water.

"What if Morgen's the one who killed Connor Townes?" Jennifer asked softly.

I stared at her. Until this second, it hadn't occurred to me that the creature we'd come here to meet could be the killer. "Why didn't you mention that earlier?" I said in a furious undertone, not wanting to be overheard by said water creature.

"I just thought of it," she admitted. Then she looked over at me. "Should we give up and go home?"

"No. We're here now. And there are two of us, plus Rafe standing by. We might not have Margaret Twigg's powers, but between us we're pretty good."

"Okay. You've got the coin?"

I pulled it from my pocket and placed it on my palm, where the silver glinted in the moonlight.

"Do we ask for the spirit to appear first or throw the coin in first?" she wondered.

"I say we call it first, then we throw the coin."

"Okay. Let's do it."

I said, "You call it, and I'll throw the coin."

She nodded, and I watched as she centered herself. I did the same, pulling strength and energy from all the nature around us. The water beneath our boat, the land on either side, the moon above, and the air soft against our skin.

Jennifer's voice was clear:

"Spirit of the river, Morgen, creature of the deep,
An audience with you we seek.
This gift is yours to keep.
With you we wish to speak."

I waited in case she wanted to say more, but there was silence. She'd finished.

This gift is yours to keep? It sounded a bit like a TV ad, but I doubt I'd have done any better. She nodded at me, and I tossed the coin. We heard a splash as metal hit water, and then there was a moment of silence when I wondered if we'd wasted our time and money. But then I started to feel something. The boat rocked slightly, and the surface of the water began to ripple.

Something was happening, and all I could think about was movies I wished now I'd never seen. Like *Jaws,* for instance. I reached out for Jen's hand and found hers seeking mine. We clung to each other as the ripples turned into a shape that rose until it was like a wave looking like a man, with water streaming from it. He had curly hair and a beard. His naked torso was muscular, the arms strong from swimming, presumably. His eyes were bold and black, though they looked like they were crying with all the water.

Normally, I associated water gods with tridents, but he was holding a long staff that looked a lot like a punting pole.

Water streamed from his head and his torso as he emerged from the water until he was waist-deep and staring at us. "Well, you got my attention, witches. What do you want?"

We looked at each other. "Thank you for coming," Jen said very politely.

He lifted the coin of Poseidon and showed it to us. "You get top-drawer service when you throw in an image of a god I much admire." He gazed down fondly at the coin, and I wondered if he was a collector, too.

He seemed very approachable, so I said, "We're

wondering if you can help us with something that happened here on the river."

"Do my best."

How did you go about asking a mythological creature if he'd murdered a mortal? It was a delicate question at the best of times, and when the two of us were sitting in a punt at night with no one around, knowing someone had recently been murdered in very similar circumstances, it seemed akin to foolhardiness. I decided to go in as softly as I could.

"A friend of ours had a bad accident here the other night."

Jen jumped in right on top of me. "Not a friend. We wouldn't call him a friend, Lucy."

Oh no, I didn't want anyone thinking Connor was any friend of ours. I amended, "Right. Not a friend. A friend of a friend. Acquaintance of a friend, really."

Morgen shifted, and the river water dipped and eddied with him. "I like to keep moving," he said. "I get cold if I stand still. Do you mind punting along, and I'll glide beside you?"

"Of course."

Neither of us had a clue about punting. Jennifer was still holding the punting pole, and once more she pushed it against the bottom of the river. But the boat went sideways and headed towards the bank. Then she went to the other side, pushed again, and we zigzagged towards the other bank. I waited for the bang.

Morgen shook his head. "You two really don't know what you're doing at all, do you?"

"Not really," Jen admitted.

He came close and put a hand under the boat. "Leave it to me, then."

To Jen, he said, "You'd better sit down."

Then it was heavenly. It was like being on a chauffeured punting boat. He drifted along beside us, and the boat glided smoothly.

I said, "We're wondering if you know anything about a man who died here the other night?"

The boat wobbled, and I felt as though a shiver of anger must have gone through him. "Polluting my river, that's what he was doing. It was horrible. He was half in and half out of the water. Nothing I could do for him."

That sounded like he hadn't killed Connor Townes. Or at least wasn't admitting to it. That emboldened me a little bit.

"Did you see any of what happened? How he died?"

Okay, he wasn't like an eyewitness you could use in court, but if we could discover what had happened, then maybe we could find a way to prove it and find Rafe's precious painting.

He said, "There was a terrible racket. That's what brought me over to start with." He scowled at the boat. "I don't like this outfit anyway. They don't pay their proper tribute. All the other ones do."

And then it hit me. "It's you, isn't it?"

"I couldn't answer that until I had more specifics," Morgen said.

"I mean, it's you who's causing all the trouble with these boats. One of the people who works for the company says the punts always come back covered in weeds or the poles are missing or—"

He began to chuckle then. And when a river god chuckled, the whole of the quiet river became suddenly turbulent. "Noticed that, did they?"

"They did. But I don't think they understood what they were doing wrong."

"That's because the serious operators here won't have let them in on the secret. And it's not up to me to tell them. We all wanted them gone. They were trouble from the beginning. Not proper river people. You can always tell. I've been here long enough to recognize the fly-by-nighters. The ones who come in for a quick buck and then are gone the minute things get difficult."

"Right, and speaking of difficult," I said, "one of their patrons died the other night. We're trying to find out how it happened."

"I can't tell you who killed him because I didn't see it. Could have been an accident. He was stupid enough and drunk enough. But I can tell you I heard shouting."

Ooh, this was good news. "Do you remember what the shouting was about?"

"Nah. Had water in my ears, didn't I."

"Was it men? Women? One man, one woman?"

"There was a woman first. Lovely thing she was, much too good for the fellow she was with. She soon realized it too, for she told him to put her onto shore. I may have helped a bit. Saw her off safely."

"That was nice of you," I said.

"It was after that I heard shouting. Fellas. A couple of them. And they sounded angry. Like I said, I didn't hear much, but one said to the drunk in the boat, 'We're in this together. Don't think about holding out.' Something to that effect. I headed up past St. Hilda's to get some peace and quiet. When I came by later, he was dead."

"But you don't know what any of it referred to."

He said, "No. And now I've helped you, I want a favor back from you." Like a two-thousand-five-hundred-year-old silver coin wasn't enough? He said, "See if you can get rid of those fools. They've no business here. If my temper gets up, I might start overturning the punts, and I wouldn't want innocents to get hurt."

Oh, great, put that pressure on us. I said, "We don't even know these people, but we'll do what we can."

I had an idea that with the police already investigating the death, the fly-by-night punting company was closing for good, but I didn't say that to our watery friend in case I was wrong.

"Right," he said, "I'll take you back to where you started. And next time you two take out a boat, I suggest you either take a lesson in how to punt or hire a chauffeur."

He was as good as his word, and this time he didn't hang beside us chatting. He went underwater, and we moved faster than probably any punt in the history of punting. It was more like a hovercraft. I had to hang on to the back of the seat, feeling the air rush through my hair, but it was exhilarating too. Honestly, when you count supernatural creatures among your friend group, it can have surprising advantages.

Just as we reached the place where we'd put in, he slowed us and set us so gently against the bank, we barely even felt it.

"Thank you," we both called after him.

By way of acknowledgement, he sent up a stream of water from the middle of the river.

We didn't want to leave the punt in the river, but the two of us weren't strong enough to haul it onto the bank. "Is it pathetic if I call Rafe?" I asked Jen.

"If you don't, I will," she said.

I used the phone mostly because I didn't want to worry

him. I felt I should only shout his name if I was in danger. He answered right away and then came down to help us. And when I say help us, he single-handedly hauled the boat onto the riverbank and then hefted it back to where we'd hired it.

We told him everything we'd found out, which wasn't much, but it did seem like those men might have killed Connor because he'd boasted to them that he had a painting to sell. Why hadn't he given it to them? Had he decided to keep all the money rather than splitting it with his partners?

"Are you too tired for the vampire knitting club tonight? If so, we can reschedule," Rafe said.

I was pretty tired from the day's sleuthing but also exhilarated about our progress. "No. I'm up for it. Are you, Jen?"

"I'm in," she said.

"Good. Lochlan's got some news. The man's remarkable. He put out the word that he was looking for royal portraits, and he's already had a hit."

I said, "That's astonishingly fast. How does he know it's not somebody who takes photographs of royal jubilees or something?"

He shook his head. "Lochlan wouldn't have called a meeting of the vampire knitting club unless he had a credible lead."

I had imagined quiet evenings with my new husband, not rushing around solving murders and finding missing paintings. Still, it was partly my fault that we'd lost the painting in the first place.

"I'm a bit chilled. Maybe we can make some tea or hot chocolate at the flat and take it down to the meeting?"

Jen supported my suggestion, and as soon as we arrived

back in Harrington Street, Rafe went into the back room and we went upstairs to make tea. Soon we were all gathered around the whiteboard once again, and once again, Lochlan was chairing this meeting. The nice thing about holding a mug of tea was that it made it impossible to knit. I was quite pleased with this arrangement.

CHAPTER 14

*L*ochlan said, "Before I tell you my news, I thought we'd check in and see how all of you did."

I was glad Jennifer and I had already had our interrogation, for want of a better word, of Tina. We had something useful to report. Even though Lochlan and Rafe had already heard about our interview, the others hadn't.

He started with Theodore. "I know you've had very little time, but have you learned anything more about Connor Townes?"

"Nothing terribly useful. He grew up in Slough, on the Britwell Estate." He turned to us. "A council housing estate built after World War II when much of London had suffered bomb damage. His father left when he was young; mother and he don't get along. She's moved to Liverpool, and recently Connor Townes moved back to Britwell Estate, where he's part of a loose organization of young ne'er-do-wells." He picked up his notebook and flipped through to his notes. "The closest that young man ever came to stealing fine art was when he 'won' a Jensen Interceptor at poker using suspicious cards."

And didn't that figure. His greatest treasure was obtained by cheating.

Then Lochlan turned to me and Jennifer. "Did you get a chance to talk to Tina?"

He already knew we had, as I'd told him and Rafe, but I thought it was nice of him to give Jennifer a chance to report. I nodded to her, and she accurately and succinctly reported what had happened and what we'd learned from Tina, which was basically that she was the one who had invited Connor Townes to the wedding.

Then she told the meeting about our punting expedition and our chat with Morgen. We really had been busy for a couple of mortals who needed a full night's sleep.

Sylvia said, "And Agnes and I have not been idle. We've got an appointment with Penelope Bruton in St. Ives. She's an expert in recovering stolen art."

"Remarkable," Lochlan said. "Well done, Sylvia."

She preened under his praise.

Then it was his turn. "And I can report that after quietly putting word out in certain circles that I'm looking for very specific royal portraits, I've been contacted."

This was pretty exciting, and of all the stuff we'd had to report tonight, nothing was going to come close to this, and we all knew it.

"Who contacted you?" Sylvia asked.

"A chap called Michael Stoltz. He owns art galleries in London, Paris, and New York. But behind this respectable front is someone who prefers not to give his name but who would like to meet me to discuss an opportunity."

I glanced over at Rafe, but he was doing his impassive thing. I wondered if I'd ever be able to cultivate that cool, impervious look and seriously doubted I would. Not if I only had one lifetime to work on it.

"Theodore, can you see what you can find out about Michael Stoltz and anyone he associates with?" Lochlan asked.

"Of course," Theodore said.

"I played the part of an exacting collector." And I thought he'd have no trouble doing that. "I said, 'Please don't waste my time. I'm currently interested in Tudor portraits, anything from Henry VII to Elizabeth I.'"

"Did he say, 'I happen to have a nice Elizabeth I that just came in'?" Jen asked, sounding super excited.

"Not quite. He said he'd get back to me and within an hour had set up a meeting in London."

This was truly exciting. "When is it?" I asked.

"I told him I'm only in town for two days. The meeting is tomorrow night."

I don't even know why I said it, but I blurted out, "Can I come?"

Everyone turned to me, looking quite surprised. Rafe most of all. But I felt like I was so invested in this whole thing, I needed to know what the next chapter of the story was.

Lochlan paused for moment and said, "Actually, that's a very good idea." He turned to Rafe. "Lucy's got skills and talents that you and I don't have. I can protect her, but she's got human insights that you and I have lost."

Also, don't forget I'm a witch. But he seemed to think me being able to read other humans was more useful. And maybe he was right.

Rafe looked concerned. "I don't know. These people are very dangerous."

Lochlan all but puffed out his chest. "Don't you think I can ensure her safety?"

There was a glance that passed between them. "I'm counting on it."

Ooh, and if anything happened to me, I didn't think Lochlan's life, undead as it was, would be worth continuing.

He seemed to understand the stakes and nodded. "Agreed."

I didn't appreciate the thought that I was going to be treated like a precious piece of china that shouldn't be dropped, but on the other hand, it was nice to know that a big, strong vampire had my back.

Rafe said, "It's me who should go to the meeting. I'm the one who's missing the painting."

"And you're the one who owns the stolen property. If these are the people who took it, you're the last person who should be in that meeting."

This was unarguably true, but Rafe still argued the point for a few minutes until Sylvia finally shut him down.

"Rafe," she said. "Lochlan won't let anything happen to Lucy. You've got to stop being so overprotective."

He was, and she'd nailed it, and as annoying as it was, I also found his urge to protect me one of his most endearing qualities.

Finally, he nodded. "But I'll be close by."

And with that compromise, we were all in agreement.

As Rafe and I drove home from Oxford, I turned to him. "You didn't mention the possibility of Dr. Pattengale having the portrait," I said.

"To be honest, this meeting with the dealer sounds more promising. I still believe Connor Townes stole the painting."

"But Connor Townes didn't know the gallery was there," I argued. Unlike Dr. Pattengale, who'd known because my dear old dad had spilled the beans.

"No. But Simon Pattengale's admission explains how Connor Townes could have discovered the existence of the gallery."

"Oh," I said, the light dawning. "You think that while Dr. Pattengale was admiring the Rembrandt, Connor Townes might have come in snooping and seen the secret gallery?"

"I do. And if those men whom Georgia claimed she heard calling to him were some of these ne'er-do-wells, as Theodore calls them, then he may have shown them the portrait and, seeing its value, they took it from him, killed him, and are now selling it."

I nodded. "And all we have to do now is get it back." I knew he was very rich, but I had to ask, "Will you buy it back?"

The car purred along for a minute or two before he answered, steel in his tone. "I don't think so."

I was exhausted when we arrived home but filled with anticipation too. I'd be going to meet a notorious art thief tomorrow night. I felt the thrill of excitement with a dash of nerves. This was the third night for my crystal ball to bathe in moonlight, and I found myself needing that time in the quiet garden to settle.

Nyx found me there, and we sat together on a stone bench, Nyx purring as I stroked her soft fur. I gazed at Artemis, half wishing she could come along to the meeting with the art dealer, carrying her bow and arrow.

~

THE NEXT DAY, Lochlan arrived after I'd finished my breakfast of smoked salmon and scrambled eggs. I poured myself a second cup of coffee, suspecting I was going to need the hit of caffeine. Rafe said, "Isn't the security system finished yet?"

"I've come about the meeting this evening. And no, it isn't." He asked what I was wearing to the meeting with the shady underworld art dealer. I'd planned to wear a little black dress and heels. He shook his head. "Everything must be designer. And I want you in expensive jewelry."

Rafe said, "I've got exactly the jewels to impress these people. Flashy and expensive."

"Good. Then we only have to buy clothes today." He glanced at his watch, but again Rafe intervened. "I'll take Lucy shopping. It will be a pleasure."

"All designer wear, remember. Top end," Lochlan said.

Rafe looked at him the way Margaret Twigg looked at me when I'd said something she considered stupid. "Of course."

"I've always wanted to act out that scene from *Pretty Woman*," I said. At Rafe's puzzled look, I shook my head. "Another movie to add to the list of must-sees for your cultural education."

There is something incredibly seductive about shopping without even looking at the price tags. Even more interesting was that Rafe had an eye for fashion. We had so much fun. I just had to remember to keep him away from the mirrors, and at the end of only a couple of hours, I had a stunning outfit to wear tonight, plus a couple of outfits for our honeymoon. Dresses I'd have drooled at in shop windows and never even have tried on, along with shoes and bags.

When the time grew closer to leave, Rafe said, "You don't have to go, Lucy. Lochlan is perfectly capable of buying stolen art without you."

"I want to do this. It was my cousin who invited Connor Townes, and if he stole that painting, I want to help get it back." I was both thrilled and terrified at the same time. I knew I'd be safe with Lochlan, but honestly I wished that there was a way Rafe could be at the meeting. However, I knew he'd be close at hand. All I had to do was let out a squeak and he'd be there to save me. Not that I had any intention of squeaking. If this art dealer knew anything about Rafe's painting, I'd be so cool and professional, we'd have that painting in no time.

Once I was dressed in the designer outfit—a little black dress from Dior that cost an obscene amount of money, a pair of Jimmy Choos with a high heel and lots of bling, and a Prada handbag—I felt like I was playing dress-up. I laid on the makeup thicker than usual, and then the most painful part of the role I had to play was to take off my wedding and engagement rings. It really hurt me to take off those precious rings, but even Rafe agreed that if I went along as a married woman, it wouldn't look so good.

I did my hair up in a style that was more sophisticated than my usual look. When I emerged downstairs, Lochlan and Rafe both agreed I would do.

"And now for the jewels," Lochlan said.

Rafe took us into the library and opened a safe. He said, "The rubies are probably the most valuable of my collection," and reached for a leather jewelry case so old, the leather had cracked. When he opened it, I actually gasped. There was a necklace with rubies set within triangles of diamonds. When

Rafe lifted the piece out and placed it around my neck, he said, "Burmese pigeon blood rubies."

Lochlan stared at the necklace. "You got that at the Christie's auction in 1965, didn't you?"

"That sounds about right," Rafe said, lifting the gorgeous necklace from its case and clasping it around my neck, where it sat against my breastbone, cool and expensive.

"I was bidding against you. A stunning piece. I remember there was a ring that came up as a second lot. It was exquisite."

Rafe reached into the safe for a velvet ring box and flipped it open. The ruby and diamond ring was so large, I'd have thought it was costume jewelry. "Ah, you got that too," Lochlan said.

"I was in a mood," Rafe said. "Probably overpaid, but they've appreciated nicely."

Rafe slipped the ring onto my finger, and it glowed like a beating heart. Fortunately, it fit perfectly, otherwise I'd have been terrified I'd lose it. "The tiara might be a bit much," Rafe said, "but I think these earrings would work." I was still stumbling over the tiara thing when he handed me a pair of ruby and diamond drop earrings. I was so glad I'd put my hair up, as they showed beautifully.

Lochlan always dressed nicely, but even he'd upgraded to a designer jacket and trousers. His watch was so understated, it screamed wealth, and he wore a single ring with an enormous emerald.

"Shall we?" he said to me.

"Let's get Rafe's painting back," I agreed.

We set off together, but I knew Rafe wouldn't be far

behind. As we headed into London, I was so nervous, my knees kept jumping up and down.

I said, "Lochlan, what's our cover story?"

He looked at me, rather amused. "There is no cover story. They know who I am."

I couldn't believe it. "You gave them your real name?"

He shook his head at me, a bit like the way Rafe sometimes did. "Lucy, do you really think we would have a meeting with one of the most notorious thieves in the world if I'd given him a false name? It's the very fact that he knows who I am and has a faint idea of my net worth that he would even contemplate meeting with us on such short notice."

I could see that this was true, but it seemed kind of dangerous. "What about me? Are we giving my real name?" I wasn't at all sure of how I felt about that.

He hesitated for a moment and then said, "I'm going to introduce you as my associate Lucy. He doesn't need a last name."

That didn't seem right. "Won't he be curious?"

He looked at me again. "I doubt it."

And then I got it. I gasped. "You mean he'll think I'm your girlfriend?"

"It doesn't matter what he thinks. He'll look at those jewels you're wearing and know that we're not messing around."

I put a hand to the gorgeous necklace. "He won't try to steal them, will he?"

"If he tries, it'll be the last thing he does."

Right. I very much hoped this guy we were meeting with didn't try to steal my jewels. I didn't want to see his end.

We met in a discreet townhouse in Mayfair. It was the

kind of place you read about or saw on TV when they did stories about Russian oligarchs buying up London. The place was a mansion.

We were let in by a woman who acted like the house-keeper. When Lochlan gave his name, she said, "Mr. Simons is expecting you."

Mr. Simons? That seemed like such a normal name for a guy who worked the black market. And the place seemed so respectable, I started to feel disappointed. And then we were led up a set of stairs into a room that looked like a cross between a gentleman's club and an old-fashioned library. A man was sitting in a red leather club chair with a glass of something that looked like whiskey and reading a newspaper. The scent of cigar was in the room, and I could see a half-smoked one sitting in an ashtray by his side. He rose and took in the pair of us. He was a tall, thin man, wearing trousers and a white shirt with a cardigan over top. I knew enough now about knitting to know that it was not hand done, but the wool was high-quality cashmere. I bet it had been expensive.

Two men stood discreetly in two corners of the room. Bodyguards, I supposed. They remained impassive and barely glanced our way, but I felt that if we made one move out of line, they'd move pretty quickly then.

Lochlan took it all in and coolly shook the man's hand. "Lochlan Balfour, and this is my associate, Lucy."

Mr. Simons shook Lochlan's hand and said, "A pleasure to meet you. I've heard so much about you. Read about you in the business press. You're a very successful man."

Since it was a statement, not a question, Lochlan nodded in agreement.

And then he turned to me. "And Miss Lucy. What a pleasure to meet you."

And that was it? I was Miss Lucy? He seemed more interested in the jewels I was wearing than in me. As he shook my hand, I saw that on his bony hand he wore diamonds too. Bigger than mine, but I bet they weren't as good a quality. And then he ushered us to two chairs and offered us both a drink.

Lochlan took a whiskey, but on instinct, I crossed my legs and said, "I'd like some champagne."

He chuckled at that. And I thought I'd hit the note just right. I mean, if I was going to be treated like a floozy, I might as well act like one. He made the tiniest motion with his head, and one of the stooges disappeared. A few minutes later, the housekeeper came back with a tray, and on it was a bottle of champagne in ice and a crystal flute. Meanwhile, Mr. Simons had poured Lochlan a whiskey. He offered him a cigar, but Lochlan declined.

The stooge was now back in his corner, and the stage was set for the next act.

I was almost too nervous to sip my champagne, but at least it gave me something to do. I was pleased to notice my hands weren't shaking, and when the diamonds and rubies caught the light, I let myself enjoy the sparkle.

Mr. Simons said, "We are both busy men. I won't waste time on small talk. You're an art collector, I see."

Lochlan nodded. "I have an interest in portraits of the Tudor monarchs."

"An interesting field. Not so much available, of course. And most of it is in public collections, as I'm sure you know."

"I'm looking for something a little more exclusive."

"Naturally. Why don't you tell me what you have in mind, and I'll see if I can't obtain it for you? And is there a particular Tudor you're interested in?" Mr. Simons asked.

"Yes. The Virgin Queen."

If the man was surprised, he showed no sign of it. "Elizabeth I. Not so many of those around."

"I'm aware of that. I expect that's where you come in."

"What? You think this is Sotheby's Auction House, perhaps?" He chuckled at his own humor. Lochlan gave a slight smile, and I, feeling trapped between them, gave a slightly wider smile.

"This wouldn't be in the public market."

"It won't be easy either. I know of only three portraits of Queen Elizabeth that aren't in major galleries. One in Saudi Arabia, you can forget about that one; one in New York; and one in Scotland. I could get either of those two for you. Ten million pounds."

Lochlan leaned back and crossed his legs at the ankle. "For ten million pounds, I'd expect you to get the Darnley portrait out of the National Gallery."

This time, both men chuckled, and I felt brave enough to join in.

"And that's all there are? Only three existing portraits in the world in private collections?"

"Unless you know something I don't know. You got a line on one, I'll see what I can do."

"No. You're the expert."

He took a sip of his whiskey. He said, "I want provenance and more information on the portraits you can get me. And I'll pay five million pounds."

A healthy bit of haggling ensued, and at the end, they'd agreed on a price of eight million pounds.

I am not kidding. Eight million pounds for a painting that other people owned. They both acted like this kind of stuff happened all the time.

They shook hands again, and Mr. Simons said, "I'll need half up front before I set about acquiring your portrait."

Lochlan said, "I'll be in touch."

And then we left. And that was it.

I didn't say a word until we'd been shown out of the house and were back in the car heading away, and then I said, "He didn't know anything about Rafe's portrait, did he?"

"Unless he was playing with us, no."

I thought for a minute. "Is that good news or bad news?"

"I'm not sure. If Rafe's Elizabeth was floating out there on the open market, I would have simply bought it back."

"But it isn't. What does that mean?"

"The way I see it, it either means that whoever stole it has no intention of selling it, or the thief hasn't made their next move yet."

I really hoped it was the latter.

But the disappointing thing was we were no closer to finding Rafe's stolen painting.

Now what?

CHAPTER 15

*W*e got back to Rafe's manor house for a debrief. Lochlan and I shared with him everything we'd learned at the meeting with the art thief. It wasn't in his nature to look disappointed—I imagined he'd experienced plenty of disappointment in his time on earth—but I would have liked him to look pleased, relieved, at least to have felt that we had a lead. But we had nothing.

No, Lochlan argued, we had something. He said, "If the painting was on the market, we'd know about it. And there's one other thing: It's always good to know that art thieves aren't aware that you own an Elizabethan portrait."

Rafe didn't look relieved by this news. "If it's out there somewhere, chances are they're going to find out."

Lochlan said, "Not if we get it back before word gets out. I've got my not inconsiderable resources working on this. If it's out there, we'll get it back."

Rafe said, "What if it fell out of Connor Townes's pocket when he fell in the river?"

Lochlan gave this serious thought. "That wouldn't be ideal. Should we get some divers down in the river looking?"

"It crossed my mind."

I had no idea what kind of damage could be done to a five-hundred-year-old painting if it spent any time in the River Cherwell, but I didn't imagine it would be the best thing for it. I felt so guilty, I could hardly stand it. And maybe my guilt made me think a bit harder.

I said, "What happened to Connor's car?"

They both looked at me. It was one of those obvious things that none of us had thought of yet. I continued, "He kept bragging to everybody about his Jensen Interceptor and how few of them were made."

"You're right. He did," Lochlan said. Not that Lochlan had been talking to Connor Townes, but we'd all gone over all the conversations with people who had seen the man on his last day on earth.

Lochlan said, "The woman he left the wedding with said he drove them to the river, but did she say where they parked?"

I shook my head. "I'm pretty sure Georgia just said a secluded spot."

He turned to Rafe. "What about the police? Have they found the car?"

Rafe shook his head. "It's not in any of the police reports."

"They'd have looked for it, surely?"

Rafe said, "Let me check with my sources. I'll get back to you on that."

I was starting to feel excited. This might be the best lead we had. I said, trying not to be too eager, "It makes sense, right? He steals the painting, maybe hides it in the glove compartment, and then drives off. For all we know, it's still in the glove compartment of his car."

"And the police don't know about the missing painting, so they'd have no reason to search his car. Maybe they haven't even thought to look for it. Until somebody complains about a car that's been sitting unclaimed for days, it might just get overlooked."

It was getting late now, but I knew a bunch of creatures who'd be only too happy to go snooping around Oxford late at night searching for a car. I mean, they went cruising around Oxford late at night anyway. At least this would give them a specific purpose.

Lochlan said, "I don't want you two to get your hopes up too high, but it's a lead. I'll go and have a word with Theodore and Alfred and some of the others. We'll form a search party. If that car is there, we'll find it tonight."

Rafe said, "You'll let us know as soon as you find anything?"

"Believe me, you'll be the first to know."

Lochlan went off, and I went over to Rafe and threw my arms around him. "I am so sorry," I said.

He put me away from him and looked down into my face. "What are you sorry about?"

"I never meant for you to lose something so valuable."

It was his turn to pull me to him. "I've gained something so much more valuable, my dear."

I HAD such high hopes that Lochlan would turn up Connor's Jensen Interceptor and find Rafe's painting perfectly unharmed. Unfortunately, when morning came and there was still no word, we sat down to a rather glum breakfast. William tried his best, making me American pancakes exactly the way I liked them, with crispy bacon and real maple syrup. Rafe had his usual breakfast.

I said, "Maybe Lochlan didn't want to bother us too early."

"Perhaps," Rafe said, but I could tell he didn't believe it any more than I did.

We'd finished breakfast and I was enjoying a second cup of coffee out on the terrace when Lochlan and Jennifer showed up.

Lochlan said, "It's bad news, I'm afraid," as though we hadn't worked that out from his expression and Jennifer's. "We looked everywhere. If that car was in the vicinity of the river, if it was anywhere in Oxford, we'd have found it."

"But where could it be?" I asked.

Jennifer said, "We were talking about that. Don't you think those guys that got Connor the great deal on the punting boats might have found it first?"

My heart sank. "You think they know that there's a price-less treasure inside it?"

Lochlan said, "I'm more worried that they've sold it."

"No," I moaned. Rafe looked pretty glum. He said, "Do you have any idea how many treasures throughout history have been lost for stupider reasons than this? Perhaps it's gone to a chop shop. Or somebody will just go through the car and toss everything in a bin, not having a clue what they have in their hands."

I said, "It's only been a few days. Even if they sold the car, we should be able to find out who they sold it to." I turned to

Lochlan. "Couldn't you and some of your associates go and visit Jason Smith and his buddies? I'm sure if you asked them in the right way, they would tell you what happened to that car."

"Oh, believe me, I thought of it. They're nowhere to be found. They've disappeared. Left Oxford, certainly, with no forwarding address. Even Jason Smith's great-aunt doesn't know where they are. Once the police started sniffing around, they were gone."

"Do you think they took the car with them?"

"If it's in this country, we'll find it."

I had full confidence that he would, but the question was, would that painting still be in the car? Assuming it ever had been?

William got Jennifer some coffee, and the four of us sat outside. I was thinking madly, hoping that caffeine might prod my brain into action. Jennifer seemed to be doing the same.

Suddenly, she said, "Are we focusing too much on Connor Townes having stolen the painting?"

We all turned to look at her. She had an expression that was like you get when you feel like you could be saying something stupid but it's worth taking the chance in case what you have to say is actually important. I knew that look well because I was pretty sure it was on my face a lot of the time when I was trying to figure out who was at the bottom of a murder.

She said, "We don't even know for sure that Connor took it."

Which would kind of be a bit of a relief since it meant that the painting probably wasn't at the bottom of the Cherwell, and probably not in the glove compartment of a car that had been sold who knew where. However, it still left a pretty big pool of possibilities as to where the painting actually was.

Lochlan nodded. "You make a good point, Jennifer. We have focused quite narrowly. What are the other possibilities?"

Apart from a lot of mortals at the wedding, Dr. Pattengale came to mind. I hated throwing my dad's friend under the bus, but the doctor admitted he'd been in that room and looked behind the panels. I related all this even though everybody here knew it.

I said, "I can't imagine that my dad's friend would steal a painting, but what if he did? What if he suddenly went a bit crazy and thought how much he'd love to have a portrait of Queen Elizabeth? And let's say he picked it up in a moment of madness, slipped it in his pocket or his wife's purse, and he still has it?"

"It's a bit of a stretch, don't you think?" Lochlan said.

"Yes. I do. I also think it's a possibility worth checking out."

Rafe said, "I hoped Connor's car would turn up with the painting in it. Since we haven't located the car, I do plan to search the doctor's home."

"I've got specialists for this kind of search. We could be in and out in an hour, and no one would ever know we were there," Lochlan said.

Rafe said, "I'm coming with you."

"Do it tonight. I'll get hold of my parents and make some excuse as to why they should take their friends out again. It shouldn't be that hard."

"And we're leaving tonight," Jennifer told me. "That's why

I came. To say goodbye. Sylvia has an appointment with the art expert in St. Ives tomorrow."

"I'm going to miss you," I said, "but I'll see you as soon as we come down to Cornwall."

Jen said, "You know, I was thinking. Tina might know something about Connor's associates. I mean, if she held onto stuff for him and hung around whenever he let her, don't you think she might have met them or at least have names or an idea of where they might go?"

I glanced at Rafe and Lochlan, but neither of them looked like Jen had cracked the case. However, we didn't have any better leads. "But Tina and her parents left this morning." I knew because Rafe had settled their bill.

"I was thinking I could stop in on our way to Cornwall," Jennifer said. "I looked up Tina's address in the database for wedding invitations at your shop. She lives in a place called Sidmouth."

I shook my head. "It's one of the weird things about England you're going to have get used to. Hardly anything is spelled the way it sounds. It's *Sidmuth*. My favorite is a village in Cornwall, which sounds like it's spelled M-U-Z-Z-L-E, but it's actually M-O-U-S-E-H-O-L-E."

"Mousehole?"

"Right, but pronounced *Muzzle*. Who knows why."

One of the best things about having another North American around was being able to say things like this without causing offense. Of course, I might be able to pronounce it, but I didn't know where Sidmouth was. We looked on a map and discovered that Sidmouth was on the Devon coast, near Lyme Regis. It was described as a pretty coastal town popular with retirees. The perfect place for Tina's mom and dad to retire, but I wondered what Tina did there. She had her own address, but I wondered if she actually spent a lot of time with her parents. She didn't seem like someone who had a lot of friends.

We were looking at the map when Jennifer pointed out the obvious. "Sidmouth is sort of on the way to Cornwall."

While that wasn't exactly true, it was definitely in the right direction.

She said, "I'm sure your grandmother and Sylvia won't mind stopping, and I can run in and ask Tina if she knows where Jason Smith and his buddies went. She must know something that would give us a clue to where your painting is."

It was great to be able to split the load of work. I was quite enthusiastic about this idea. But I warned her that Gran had to stay out of sight as Tina knew she was dead. And Sylvia could be difficult.

She said, "Don't worry, I've already figured that out. I'll find a way to make her come up with the idea herself."

Jen was catching on.

I DON'T KNOW how she did it, but true to her word, Jen managed to get Sylvia to come up with the idea of Jen stopping in to see my cousin Tina on the way to Cornwall. I didn't think Sylvia cared too much about who killed Connor Townes, but she could totally get behind Rafe's desire to get his precious painting back.

She was obviously pleased with herself about her appointment with the art expert, and I could see she was excited to be moving to Cornwall. Maybe she'd had enough of Oxford too.

They left that evening from Harrington Street, and I was there to say goodbye, along with Nyx.

They'd chosen five p.m. for their departure time as a compromise between vampire time and human. Jen wanted to visit Tina on the way, and as Alfred calculated it would take them three hours to drive to Sidmouth, they couldn't show up much after eight and call it a social visit. Then it was another three hours to get to Rafe's house in Cornwall. I hoped Jen could sleep in the car. Otherwise she'd be exhausted when she arrived.

The store was shut and we stood in the shade, but even so, Gran wore a big hat. I didn't think anyone would recognize her as there were so few people on the street, but still, I kept an eye out. As sad as I was to see my gran make this move, it was stressful staying constantly vigilant.

Sylvia and Gran had decided to leave most of their things here until they figured out what they wanted to ship down to their new home. Even so, there was a hefty amount of luggage being loaded into the Bentley. "Be careful of my hat trunk," Sylvia warned Alfred, who was loading the bags. Her hat trunk was vintage Louis Vuitton, and there was a matching steamer trunk that had no doubt made many a voyage in her heyday, as well as a couple of suitcases. This was Sylvia traveling light.

My grandmother had one suitcase, a blue Samsonite from the 1970s that I remembered from the times she'd come to visit us when I was a kid. She looked much more unsure about the move. We hugged each other, and I felt like this was the end of an era. I tried not to get weepy, but I was truly sad to say goodbye to my gran. So much had changed since I'd arrived here a little lost, a little brokenhearted, and with no idea of my own powers or that my beloved grandmother was not the grandmother I had always known.

I tried to cheer us both up. "We'll be down to Cornwall ourselves in a few days. And you know I'll come down there lots to visit you."

Gran nodded, but I could see she was sad to leave me and Oxford. She hugged me tight. "You look after yourself, my love. And I'll see you very soon."

"I will. And don't worry about the shop, it's in good hands."

She nodded. "I know. And I'm always close by if you need advice." Then she looked back at Cardinal Woolsey's. It looked particularly nice with the new window display that my cousin Violet had created. As sad as Gran was, I was sad too. This place had always been my refuge and she'd always been here. To think of her far away, even only as far as Cornwall, seemed like, I don't know, a new chapter was opening. I suppose me getting married was a big part of that, too. Things were changing.

I hugged her hard. "I'll see you in a few days."

Sylvia snapped. "Honestly, girl, it's your honeymoon. We don't want to see you for at least a week."

My grandmother nodded. "And two would be better." Then Gran voiced the words I hadn't said. "But it won't be the same. I'm going to miss you and dear Cardinal Woolsey's." She glanced into the window of the closed shop at the basket of wool where Nyx sometimes slept. "And, though I can no longer see them or talk to them, I'll miss all our lovely customers."

"I know. But remember, you're going to open another knitting shop in Cornwall. And now you'll be able to interact with people and go out in the day if you want to." I'd talked about this at length with Rafe and Sylvia and even Gran herself. Yes, there was a slight risk that someone from Oxford might end up in a Cornish knitting shop and recognize Gran, but the chances were a lot slimmer than if she stayed here. Besides, there was always that forgetting spell. And the longer time went on, the less people were likely to connect the woman who used to run Cardinal Woolsey's with a woman working in a shop in Cornwall. At least that's what we all hoped. For now, I was breathing a sigh of relief mixed with sadness that my gran wouldn't be freaking me out by forgetting she wasn't supposed to be seen locally by people who'd known her when she was fully alive. I would miss her, though.

"No, not that one," Sylvia said sharply as Alfred prepared to hoist a smaller bag into the car. "I'll carry that one on my lap." In a softer tone, she said, "It's my jewel case."

He handed it to her and said, "What did your last servant die of?"

"A pain in the neck," she said, and that made them both laugh. I was less amused. Vampire humor isn't to everyone's taste.

Holding her monogrammed jewelry case that was bigger than my overnight bag, Sylvia turned to me. "Goodbye, Lucy. We'll do our best to find a good location for our next knitting shop. We'll see you soon." And with a brisk hug, she turned and slid into the back of the car.

Alfred, who'd have been sweating heavily if he were still mortal, gave me a wave. "Cheerio, Lucy. See you soon." He'd spend a few days in Cornwall and then return to Oxford. At least, that was the current plan.

Gran had the mosaic bag she'd made hooked over her wrist. She'd finished it, of course and it was perfect. Before she got into the car, she handed it to me. "I hope you'll use this as your knitting bag and think of me when you do."

The bag was heavy. There was more than knitting inside.

"I've made you a double batch of your favorite gingersnap cookies. I know you won't need them, not with the way William cooks. But I wanted you to have something that would remind you of me."

I was thrilled as I peeked inside. "Gran, no one makes gingersnaps like you do. And I love the bag."

She looked very pleased. Even more pleased when I couldn't even wait until she got into the car. I had to pry off the lid of the cookie tin and sample one of the gingersnaps. I passed one to Jen and told her to make sure my gran kept her hand in by making her some when they got down south.

She crunched down on her cookie and then moaned. "Oh, wow, these are good. I am definitely going to keep reminding you until you make me some too," she said to Gran, who was already looking more cheerful.

She leaned down to pet Nyx and said, "Look after Lucy for me."

Nyx began to purr, which I took to mean, "I will."

Gran got into the car as effortlessly as a teenager. Then I turned to say goodbye to Jen.

"Thank you so much for coming and supporting me at my wedding. You were the perfect bridesmaid. Exactly the way we dreamed of our weddings when we were kids."

We hugged, and she said, "It was even more beautiful than we imagined."

"It was a great wedding, wasn't it?" If you skipped the guy falling out of the window thing and the unfortunate aftermath.

"Perfect," agreed my loyal friend.

"And when you get married, you know I'll be there."

She shook her head. "The way my love life's going, that won't be anytime soon."

"You never know. That's the great thing about love. It surprises you when you least expect it."

"You're such an optimist. I love that about you."

"I'm going to miss you," I said. Probably not for the first time.

"Me too. You have to come over to the States more, and I'm going to start coming over to see you more often. You're my bestie, I hate not seeing you every day."

Sylvia, who was much less sentimental than we were, said, "And when you come down to Cornwall for your honeymoon, she'll still be there." She glanced at Gran, who was looking at me from the car, as emotional as a vampire can be, and said, "And don't you start enacting a tragedy in five acts, Agnes. Your granddaughter will be down to see you very soon."

Sylvia doesn't have a lot of patience, so we finished our goodbyes. Just before Jen got into the Bentley, she said, "Wish me luck in Sidmouth." She even pronounced it right.

"Absolutely. Tell me if you find out anything from Tina." It was a long shot that Tina might have more information about the guys who'd run the punting operation, but we were following up every scant clue in hopes of discovering Rafe's painting.

She nodded and popped the last of her cookie into her mouth. "I will. And don't be a stranger, okay? Keep me updated on whatever you find up here."

"Sure. Hopefully this will all be over soon and then Rafe and I will be headed down your way."

"And then you'll be able to start your honeymoon." She made a face. "And at some point, I guess I better think about going home and getting a job."

I was absolutely not ready to lose my best friend. I said, "But not yet. Promise me."

She nodded. "Not yet. I'm having much too good a time to rush off. Besides, I want to see how this mystery ends."

And didn't we all.

CHAPTER 16

*S*he got in, and Alfred slowly drove the Bentley away from Harrington Street while I stood waving until it turned the corner.

Because I didn't know what else to do with myself, I went into the shop. Nyx seemed to know that I needed some extra love, for she bumped her head against my leg. I picked her up and buried my face in her soft fur.

"I'm going to miss them. I guess you will, too."

She bumped her head against my chin.

"We've got a new life now," I reminded both of us. Still, Cardinal Woolsey's would always be part of me, and I still planned to run the shop and work here at least a couple of days a week. Violet was getting more confident all the time and was a much better knitter, so I had full confidence in her ability to run the shop when I wasn't there.

I put Nyx in my little red car and drove us both home. It was still strange to think of Rafe's manor house as my home, but it was now. And it was going to take me a while to get used to not only the luxury and the space but having staff.

Not that there was anything servant-like about William or his sister. They were more like family. But they did so much for us, and William brought in people to do the housecleaning and wash windows and do all the maintenance. I had almost no housework to do. It was fantastic.

When I drove into the courtyard in front of the manor house, Henri was waiting like a pet who feels it's been left too long by its people. After I'd given him his treat and he'd waddled off, I let myself into the house, not ringing the bell as I used to do. William must have been listening for me because he appeared in the hallway.

"Lucy. I was hoping to have a word with you. Do you have a minute?"

"Of course." I hoped it wasn't anything awful. Had I done something bad or screwed up somehow? This might be my home, but I still wanted to treat the place right. I followed him into the kitchen and found a laptop open on the breakfast bar and a notepad beside it.

He said, "I was just doing some menu planning. Now that Crosyer Manor has a mistress, naturally, I'll be cooking for you."

I didn't know who was more thrilled about this news, him or me. For William, he'd been cooking all this time just for himself and his sister and then on a bigger scale for his catering clients. I knew he loved it when I was here, as it gave him somebody else to cook for.

I said, "Honestly, everything you make is fantastic."

He smiled at the compliment. "Be that as it may, it behooves me to make sure that the lady of the house oversees all the menus."

Maybe he wasn't hundreds of years old like Rafe, but he'd

been hanging around a vampire who was, so I let the lady of the house business slide. Besides, it was kind of fun being the lady of the manor, even if I was a thirty-year-old American.

I put the tin of cookies down on the marble countertop and told him they were my favorite cookies from my grandmother. Then I looked over his shoulder at the plan, and honestly my mouth started watering just looking at some of the meals he'd designed for us.

He said, "I know you're partial to pasta, and now that it's summer, I've tried to introduce more fruits and vegetables and some lighter meals. Lots of salads and things."

I thought everything looked spectacular, and I told him so.

"I'll get some proper supplies organized for the Cornwall house. I've no idea what's there."

I said, "You aren't coming on our honeymoon with us, are you?"

He looked a bit sheepish. "Rafe likes me to be there. I take care of his food."

"Of course." William was so much a part of the family, I didn't think it would even be weird to have him on our honeymoon. So I thanked him and left to find Rafe. I found him with Lochlan in the billiards room. I heard the knocking of the balls and followed the sound.

I greeted them both and then said, hesitantly, "Is there any news?"

Lochlan looked perturbed. "In spite of all my resources, we haven't yet discovered the whereabouts of the men who ran that punting operation. They're obviously staying out of sight, maybe even using aliases. But we'll find them."

I said, "Well, Jen's on her way to Sidmouth, so maybe Tina

knows something." It seemed like a pretty poor lead, but it was all I had to offer.

Rafe said, "So they got off okay?"

"Yes." Then I grinned. "Sylvia insisted on taking all her jewelry with her. There was hardly room for anything else in the car."

He chuckled. "She does like to travel in style." He added, "I know you're sad about your grandmother leaving. And if it doesn't work out and you want her to come back, you can consider it done."

I was so happy that I went over and hugged him. "Thank you for understanding. I know it's the right thing for her. I'm still a little sad."

Lochlan said, "As soon as we get Rafe's painting back, I'll head back to Ireland, and you two can get off on your honeymoon."

Rafe said, "Truthfully, I'm not sure we'll ever find that painting. I have a feeling that if it was going to turn up, it would have surfaced by now."

Lochlan didn't immediately deny what he was saying, so I supposed he was thinking the same thing. All he said was, "We haven't finished investigating yet. Let's give it a few more days."

Rafe nodded, and then I left them to finish their game.

Dinner was lasagna for me, yum, and Lochlan and Rafe joined me in the dining room. They'd been talking about security for the perimeter of the property and after dinner went off together to figure out what they wanted to do.

I headed into the lounge and found Nyx asleep on the couch. William brought in tea with two of my grandmother's cookies on a pretty china plate.

He said, "I hope you don't mind, Lucy. I took the liberty of tasting one of your grandmother's ginger biscuits. I have to say they are superb."

If even he thought they were great, then I knew I wasn't biased because they were made by my grandmother. "I know. We'll have to see if she'll give you the recipe."

He shook his head. "If I know your grandmother, she's going to keep that recipe secret so that you'll always have to go to Cornwall to get a new supply." I laughed, but I was pretty sure he was right. "However, I'll do some experimenting of my own. Let's see what I can come up with."

"You are on."

Having finished my tea and cookies, I found myself a little restless. I glanced up to find that Nyx was staring at me. She'd woken from her nap, and it seemed like she was feeling restless too. I thought maybe if I took my crystal ball outside, it would give me something to do. Margaret Twigg was going to ask me every time I saw her if I'd been working with it, so I might as well get started. Besides, it was a beautiful tool of my craft and had already proved to foretell the future.

After three nights in the moonlight, the ball was fully charged. I headed out to the cottage I'd repurposed as my witch's studio.

When I got to the stone outbuilding, I realized that Nyx had followed me. And she continued to follow me as I headed back outside and into the walled garden again, feeling instinctively that this was where I wanted to be. It was so beautiful here, so peaceful. The moon was rising, and a gentle breeze stirred the roses and carried the faint scents of rose and lavender, even a touch of rosemary.

Artemis looked on as I took the crystal ball out of its

velvet bag, and it sounds strange to say but it felt almost warm in my hand. I set it on the sundial, and Nyx jumped up on the other side of the sundial. I didn't know if I was making her restless or she was doing it to me. She put her nose almost against the crystal ball and stared into it. She was so adorable.

I said, "Can you see something in there?"

Then I leaned down and looked into it too. There was definitely something going on in there. It was like a shifting of different colored lights. I mean, we'd had two very clear nights, which in England was saying something. It must have been super bathed in moonlight.

I gazed into it and tried to remember everything Margaret had told me. Clearing my mind, relaxing my gaze. It wasn't like I was telling anyone's fortune. I was just having a peek to see if the ball had anything it wanted to tell me.

Margaret Twigg had said I could hold a question in my mind. Naturally the question I had was where was Rafe's painting, though I was enough of a witch to know that a crystal ball was unlikely to deliver me a treasure map with an X marking the spot. The clues we received were usually more cryptic than that. Still, I'd take any help I could get.

But as I relaxed my mind and my gaze, I started thinking about Jennifer. She just popped into my head, and so I went with it. Without really formulating a question, I was wondering about Jennifer's future.

She was in a transition in her life, and I wondered if I might find some clues that could help her find her path.

I was so happy in my own life, but I'd come here in transition too. I'd come a long way from the woman who'd arrived here in Oxford so lost and brokenhearted. I was now a reasonably successful business owner and a new wife married to the groom of my dreams.

Jen was in a similar situation to where I'd been when I arrived in Oxford. I hoped that she'd find her path and that it would be a smooth one. When I was thinking these thoughts, I suddenly had a picture of Jennifer at the seaside. I could see the waves pounding, and I wondered if it meant she was destined to stay in Cornwall? Though there was nothing in the crystal ball that said, "Hey, this is Cornwall." I knew it was her, though. I could see her dark hair waving in the wind. I could almost feel the cold wind of the ocean stinging my eyelids, so closely did I identify with that image. She looked content. She turned to look behind her, laughing, and I knew there was someone else. A man? A child? I felt her love for this person so much, my heart quickened.

Then the image faded.

There was a shift in the crystal ball, and then I felt a terrible coldness steal over me. A voice, icy cold and sounding a little bit like Margaret Twigg, seemed to say into my mind, "She's in terrible danger. Time is running out."

I was so shocked I lost that dreamlike state and stared into the ball. I just had a brief glimpse of a woman lying face-down, her hair streaming around her. She wasn't moving. How had the beautiful image morphed so quickly into this dark and terrible picture?

Had something happened as I was looking into the crystal ball?

"But where is she?" I asked aloud, hearing the urgency in my own voice. "Please. Tell me where she is. How can I save her?"

But the vision faded as quickly as it had appeared, and

now there was nothing to see in the ball but what looked like wispy clouds.

I glanced at my watch. It was 9:15 p.m.

I stared at Nyx, and she stared back. And then she leapt off the sundial and began to run towards the house. I grabbed the ball, shoved it in the velvet bag with no kind of finesse whatsoever, and ran after her. I was breathless by the time I roared into the house yelling for Rafe. The house had never seemed so big and empty and impossible to find someone when you needed them.

No one was in the billiards room.

"Rafe!" I ran. If I couldn't find him, I'd just have to grab my keys, take my own car, and try to find Jen using my wits, my crystal ball, and Nyx.

CHAPTER 17

I knew she'd gone towards Sidmouth, and I also knew there was no time to waste. I ran to our bedroom. Shoes, car keys, phone. I was so panicked, I could barely think straight. And every couple of steps, I'd yell Rafe's name again. What had happened to his supersonic vampire hearing?

I grabbed my phone and called Jen. She didn't answer. Then I texted her. "Please call me."

Then I called my grandmother, and Sylvia, then Alfred. Not one of them picked up.

I felt as ragey as Tina had when her phone had disappeared. What was the point of having a mobile telephone if no one answered theirs?

While I was redialing Jen, Rafe ran into the room. "Lucy. What's going on? I was at the other end of the estate. Are you hurt?"

"No. I'm fine. It's Jennifer." I was so panicked, I was trying to recall where I'd put my keys, and I couldn't seem to remember. "She's in trouble, Rafe. We have to go to her."

He put his hands on my shoulders and turned me to him. His calmness and the coolness of his fingers helped me to find my center again.

"You won't help her getting in a panic," he said calmly and clearly. I gazed into his eyes, and that helped too. I took a deep breath.

He said, "That's better. Now tell me what's happened."

"I don't know." And then I explained about the crystal ball and my vision.

"And it gave you no clues as to her location?"

"No. She was lying down. It looked like a stone floor or cement floor or something, maybe sand. She was heading for Sidmouth with Gran and Sylvia." I had a terrible thought. "Could they have had a car accident?" Was Jen on the side of the road somewhere?

"Unlikely. One of the vampires would have let you know if they'd had an accident. There's no point speculating. We'll go now. Try your grandmother again."

I started to calm down a little bit. He was right. Maybe I was overreacting or the ball was faulty. But the sick feeling inside me didn't ease.

"I don't even know where they are. They headed out hours ago. Jen's probably been to see Tina. Maybe Tina told her where those guys are. Maybe that's where Jen and the three vampires are now."

"Then Tina will tell us the same thing she told Jen and we'll follow their trail."

"Okay," I said. "I can be calm." But fear beat at my ribs all the same.

"Good. And you won't need car keys. We're taking the helicopter."

I had not even recalled in my panicked state that a car wasn't our only option. The relief that washed over me was intense. "How long will it take us to get there?"

"We'll be in Sidmouth within half an hour. Maybe throw a few things in an overnight bag in case we have to stay down there."

I nodded, so glad that he was thinking clearly, because I certainly wasn't. Nyx was on the bed staring from one to the other of us as though following the conversation, which she probably was. Rafe left in a few long strides, and in a daze I grabbed a toothbrush and a comb and threw a few things in a bag. I had no idea what I was even doing.

Then I followed in Rafe's wake, running outside, Nyx scampering beside me. When I got to the helicopter pad, I heard the low thrum of the motor. Nyx was still beside me, and somehow I knew that my familiar was meant to come with me on this trip. So I scooped her up and made my careful way to the helicopter. It held four people, and to my surprise when I got there, I saw Lochlan running towards us from the other direction. Rafe glanced at me in an unspoken question, and I nodded. I couldn't imagine anybody more useful than Lochlan Balfour in a crisis. And I had a sneaking feeling that we were heading for one. I just hoped we wouldn't be too late.

I climbed into the back with Nyx, and Lochlan settled in the front seat beside Rafe. If Rafe needed an extra set of eyes, vampire eyes were going to be a lot more useful than mine. And then the doors closed. I snapped my seat belt into place, held Nyx on my lap, and then we were rising. Normally I'd have been excited just to be in a helicopter, but right now all I could think about was getting to Jennifer. And before it was too late.

As we sailed through the air, I had a momentary memory of Nyx and me on our broomstick flying through the night. She gave me a look, and I could tell she was recalling it too.

I said, "But we couldn't have gone at this speed." Still, I needed to keep practicing. Like all my witch skills, the broom-riding was getting a bit rusty. Not that it was something I wanted to spend a lot of time doing anyway, but there were times...

And then, before I could believe it, the helicopter was lowering towards the ground. I saw benches and a garbage can and realized we were in a park, but it was nearly ten and there was no one there. Not even a stray dog walker. I had no idea if you were allowed to park helicopters in public parks, and right now I didn't much care. Lochlan helped me out and pointed. "Tina's house is that one, with the light in the window."

I was happy there was a light, as I was going to be paying my cousin Tina a visit.

I was about to head in that direction when my phone rang. It was my grandmother.

"Lucy," she said, sounding anything but traumatized. "What a lovely surprise to hear from you. How are you, dear?"

She sounded so totally fine, I had a horrible feeling that Margaret Twigg had given me a trick crystal ball. Wouldn't that be just like her? To give me something that kept sending me panicked messages that weren't true. But somehow that icy feeling in my stomach suggested that something really was going on.

I said, "Can I speak to Jennifer? I haven't been able to reach her."

"Jennifer? But she's not here, dear. We dropped her off at Tina's and we've gone to visit friends here in Sidmouth. It's very beautiful. I haven't been here for years. Jen said she'd call when she wanted to be picked up. Shall I tell her you rang?"

Clearly my grandmother did not hear the urgency in my tone, and I was just as glad to leave it that way. I had two extremely competent vampires with me. I didn't need three more.

I said, with the best assumption of ease I could manage, "That's okay. It wasn't important. I'll try her again. Talk to you soon."

And then I rang off.

I said, "They dropped her off at Tina's. I don't even know if she's still there."

"Well, we'll start there," Rafe said.

I said, "I think it's better if I go in alone."

"Absolutely not," Rafe said. "How do we know that Tina isn't the one who's endangered Jennifer? I'm not sending you into danger, Lucy."

As much as I appreciated the husbandly sentiment, I argued, "Rafe, what's one mortal woman going to do against a witch? I'm sure she just gave Jennifer some information about where Jason Smith and his gang are." Then I had a horrible thought. "Maybe they're in Sidmouth. What if they used Tina the way Con did? They could be crashing at her place."

"You are not walking into danger alone," Rafe insisted.

Lochlan said, "She's right, Rafe. Lucy alone is no threat to anyone. You know she only has to make a squeak of alarm and we'll be there."

I knew Rafe wanted to argue, but he did know that. He said, "I don't like this, Lucy. Don't even think about being brave. Anything makes you uncomfortable, you call out."

"I will. With you guys having my back, I know I'm completely safe."

I'd never been to Tina's place before, but it was a small bungalow on the east side of Sidmouth. It was brick, probably built in the 1930s, with a detached garage. Everything seemed quiet.

We must have made an odd group; two tall, gorgeous vampires, me, and a cat.

"What are you going to say to Tina?" Rafe asked.

"I'll think of something."

All I cared about was finding out where Jennifer was. If Tina thought I was a weirdo, that was her problem. She probably already thought that anyway.

"What if she's not home?" Lochlan asked.

The brick bungalow didn't look exactly bursting with life, but I said, "I'm pretty sure she's home. That's her car out front." I recognized the gray Ford Mondeo my mother had described.

They stayed back out of sight, and I approached the door of Tina's house. I knocked, and for a while I thought no one was home, but after a while I heard movement inside, and then Tina opened the door. Her eyes opened wide when she saw me.

"Lucy. What are you doing here?" The "so late" was implied. I couldn't say her tone was exactly welcoming.

Before I could deliver the story I'd made up, she said,

"Don't tell me you've left your husband already," and then laughed at her bad joke.

I gave a weak smile. "Nothing that serious. We're going to Cornwall for our honeymoon, and I came down early. Jen said she was coming to see you, so I thought I'd catch up with her here."

"So you didn't come to see me, then," she said with a whine in her tone.

"No. I did. Of course." I really wasn't very good at handling my cousin. "I wanted to see you both."

She said, "Well, Jennifer isn't here. She was, but she left."

"Oh. Do you know where she went?"

"No. She was dropped off by friends. I assume they picked her up again."

There are people who lie well and people who really don't. Tina was a good liar. If I hadn't already known from talking to my grandmother that they'd left Jen here, I would have believed Tina. So I pretended I did. From the corner of my eye I noticed Nyx was nosing around and seemed happy to stay outside. She wouldn't go far and I liked knowing she was close.

"Okay. Well, since I'm here and I have driven a long way, could I have a cup of tea?"

Since she was the one who'd complained that I hadn't come to visit, she could hardly say no. She didn't look thrilled with the idea of having tea with me, but what could she do? We were related, after all. I glanced around the small house as she led the way. It was tidy and furnished with what looked like a combination of her parents' cast-off furniture and IKEA. She went to the kitchen and put the kettle on. I noticed she'd scraped more of the nail polish off her fingernails.

I said, "It's so beautiful down here. I've never been before."

She glanced up. "Sidmouth? It's all right if you're retired, I suppose."

I said, "But you found interesting work." I couldn't even remember what she did.

She turned and glared at me. "Being a dental hygienist? I could do that anywhere." She made a lot of noise getting the teapot out and banging the mugs on the counter. I really didn't feel very welcome. Then she said, "I'm sure your mother's already told you, but I only moved here because my parents helped me buy this house. Unlike some of us, I don't have a rich husband." And then she dropped the spoon on the counter, making another clatter, and leaned forward into herself. She wailed, "And I guess I never will now. Now that Connor's gone." She was on the edge of tears.

Instantly my antagonism melted. "I'm so sorry, Tina."

I knew that Jennifer would have asked this very question, but since she'd lied about where Jennifer was, I decided to ask and see what happened. "Do you have any idea what happened to his friends? The ones who ran the punting operation?"

She shook her head. "I thought they were still in Oxford until Jennifer said they weren't."

"Right. Did she stay long? I mean, I hope you at least had a nice visit."

Her shoulders went up and down in a shrug. "Yeah. Not too bad."

I glanced around, but there was no sign Jennifer had ever

been here. It didn't look as though Tina were harboring the punting operators either. I felt completely baffled. Why would Tina lie about Jennifer leaving? I felt edgy and worried about my friend. I was tempted to say forget the tea, but somewhere between Jen coming here and my conversation with Gran, Jen had disappeared. Worse, if my crystal ball was to be believed, she was in danger. And here I was waiting for a cup of tea?

Think, Lucy. Think.

I said, "It's a lovely home. It's so quiet, I wasn't even sure you were home, but then I saw your car parked outside."

"Yep. You got me. I'm here."

And the thought that was niggling suddenly came to the front of my brain. "Why don't you keep it in the garage?"

She turned and handed me a cup of tea. She hadn't bothered to ask how I liked it, just gave it to me black. I didn't really care. I thanked her and took a sip.

She took a while answering and then said, "Because Connor's Jensen Interceptor is in my garage."

I was so stunned, I jerked my hand and splashed hot tea on my fingers. Ouch.

"You've got Connor's car?"

She went belligerent then. "Why wouldn't I? I was his girlfriend. The closest he had to a wife. He'd want me to have it."

That had to be where Jennifer was. Snooping in the garage. I wondered if she'd pretended to leave and then doubled back to check out that garage. But then somewhere along the way, something had happened to her. Maybe the punting guys were in the area after all.

Tina said, "Did he ever show it to you?"

"Who? Connor?"

"Yeah. He was so proud of that car. Did he ever show it to you?"

"No."

She got a funny look on her face. "Do you want to see it?"

Was she really going to make it that easy? I wouldn't even have to sneak around and break in after she'd gone to bed?

"Yeah. I'd love to."

She grabbed her keys off a hook and said, "Come on. I can't pretend to love it as much as he did. It was his most prized possession. Now it's mine."

UNLIKE THE KIND of garages I was used to in the States, Tina's garage didn't have a door that went from inside the house. We had to go out the front door, and then she unlocked a door at the side of the detached garage and ushered me in first. I walked in, and she reached around and flipped on a light. I was momentarily disoriented. I could smell dust and engine oil. I saw the shape of a car in front of me as my eyes became accustomed.

In the instant it took me to take one step inside the garage, I felt fear and panic and rage, and they weren't mine. From somewhere nearby, Nyx growled.

I felt movement behind me, and in a split second I spun, shaping my hand as though I were about to pitch a baseball. I felt like I still had my crystal ball in my hand, that the power of the moon was with me and my own power, that of Nyx and of Jennifer, who I could tell was somewhere near. I could feel the strength and the fire and the rage, and I shot it forward with all my might at Tina.

There was a clang as the hammer she'd been holding went flying and hit the cement pathway, taking Tina with it so her back banged against the brick siding of her house. She blinked at me, dazed for a second, and then with a snarl came running at me. She didn't have any finesse, but she had at least fifty pounds on me. However, I had a power she knew nothing about, and once more I sent her back.

"Rafe," I yelled. I didn't have time to subdue Tina. I needed to get to Jennifer.

Rafe and Lochlan were there in about three seconds. Lochlan went straight to Tina, who was now screaming and swearing at me like a crazy person. He fastened her wrists behind her using plastic restraints. "Thought they might come in handy," he said when he saw my surprise. Then she turned her fury on them.

Rafe came over and pulled me to him. "You're all right, Lucy?"

"Yes. I'm fine. It's Jen I'm worried about."

Nyx came running in and went straight to the car and meowed. I ran forward and opened the car door. There was only one, long door on each side. The upholstery was black cracked leather. The front bucket seats were empty. I pulled one forward and in the back were two more bucket seats and over them my best friend was draped. "Jen," I cried.

She was gagged with a scarf and her hands tied behind her, her ankles tied with what looked like laundry-line rope.

I took the gag out of her mouth first, and she said, "I can't believe I was so stupid. She must have drugged me."

As I began to fumble with the knots on the rope, Rafe moved me aside and did the job himself.

I went back to Tina. "What did you give her?" I walked

right up and into her face. I was shaking with rage and adrenalin.

She was at a disadvantage with her hands tied behind her back, plus she had to have noticed that I'd thrown her against the wall, twice. She looked at me with barely disguised fear, and I leaned into it. "Don't make me ask you again," I said. Lochlan came closer, and I felt him looming over her beside me.

"Drugged her," Tina said finally. "In her tea. I get drugs from the dentist I work with. They call it conscious sedation. She could have her wisdom teeth out and not even notice." Then, seeing my expression, she said, "She'll be fine."

While Lochlan stayed with Tina, Rafe and I helped Jennifer out of the car. "I'm so sorry," I said.

Her eyes opened, and she smiled at me. "I'm okay," she said. "A bit loopy, and I could use some water."

I ran into Tina's kitchen and got a glass of water and Rafe came behind me and picked up a kitchen chair. When we returned to the garage, Jennifer was rubbing her wrists. Lochlan had brought Tina inside the garage with the rest of us, probably so the neighbors wouldn't see what was going on and get involved. We all wanted to keep this visit as discreet as possible, even if there was a helicopter parked nearby.

Jen sat in the chair Rafe provided and drank down the water thirstily. Nyx jumped into her lap and curled up. I knew how comforting my familiar could be. With her free hand Jen stroked the soft, warm fur probably without even realizing she was doing it. Nyx purred but she kept her eyes open in case she was needed.

After she'd finished her water, Jen pointed at Tina. "She was going to kill me. She killed Connor."

CHAPTER 18

"*Y*ou killed Connor?" I asked Tina. Even though she'd attacked Jennifer and tried to hurt me, I still felt shocked. She'd adored Connor.

The garage light wasn't flattering but it illuminated the scene clearly.

Tina leaned against the garage wall and her face was hard. "I loved him, and he betrayed me. He deserved to die." Then she jutted her chin at Jennifer. "And she led him on at the wedding. I watched her. And I overheard him asking her to go out on the punting boat with him. A special late-night boat ride, just the two of them." She looked suddenly like a child about to have a tantrum. "Why didn't he ask me?"

I began to understand. "Is that the moment you realized he was never going to give you what you wanted?"

"I loved him, and he didn't love me back," she wailed. "I saw him going into the house during the wedding. Then the waiter fell out of the window and a few minutes later Con came walking up from the back. Why'd he do that? He was sweating. I told him I knew he'd pushed the waiter. I wanted to help him. I was always helping him. He told me to mind my own business. He was horrible." She sniffed. "Then he ignored me and went for *your* friend. Of all the girls to choose."

I glanced at Jen but she was staring at Tina, riveted by the tale as we all were.

Tina continued and it was as though now she'd started she couldn't stop talking. "I watched them going down to his car, the one he'd driven me to the wedding in. He was leaving me there and going off with your bridesmaid. I've never been so humiliated." She was shaking now and I began to understand how fragile her ego was and how much she'd invented a story where she and Connor were in love.

My head was spinning trying to figure out how she'd managed to kill Connor and hide all the traces. Plus, she'd got her facts wrong. It wasn't Jen who'd gone out on the boat, but Georgia. Still, if she was in confession mode, I wasn't going to stop her. "So you followed them." But how? Had she borrowed her dad's car? And no one noticed?

She shook her head. "Didn't have to. I knew where they were going. I'd been with Connor when he organized the outing so I knew where the boats were kept and where they put them into the river."

Right. She hadn't needed to follow them so she hadn't seen Jen get replaced by Georgia. The pieces were starting to fall into place.

"My parents drove me back to the hotel and then I pretended to go to bed and instead I changed into jeans and a dark hoodie. I took one of the hotel bikes they keep for guests. It was the quickest and quietest way I could think of to get to the river. I'd look like a student. No one would notice me. I only planned to tell Connor and your friend what I thought of them. Maybe push them both in the river." It was what she'd said to me the morning after he was dead. That she might push him in the river. But she'd done a lot more than that.

"When I got there, she was gone," she jerked her chin toward Jen, "but he was talking to Jase, his mate who ran the punting operation." Jase must be Jason Smith, whose great-aunt owned the house where he'd stored the punts. "Con was drunk, I could hear him rambling on about how he had something that would make his fortune. Wanted to know if Jase could fence a posh painting. Said it was like something out of a museum."

I glanced at Rafe and our eyes locked. There was a shiver of tension from all of us but Tina didn't notice. "Jase said he'd ask around and call him, but Con said to leave a message with me, like usual, it was safer." She gulped and in a rush of pain, cried, "He said I was so stupid I'd never figure out what was going on."

Ouch.

"They both laughed. Laughed at me behind my back! Then Jase told him to bring the punt back as his luck obviously wasn't in with the women and he walked back off down the path. I came out of hiding to tell Con what I thought of him. He was standing, facing away from me." She faltered. "I think he was having a wee. It was so easy to pick up the pole. While he was busy zipping up his trousers, I brought the pole down on the back of his head. I...I only wanted to teach him a lesson. I didn't think he'd die."

Whether that was true or not I couldn't tell. But Connor had died. And then she'd tried to kill my best friend. And me.

Wait. Something was missing in her story. "But you went through his pockets for his car keys."

She glared at me now and her 'poor me' routine faltered. That belligerent expression I was accustomed to returned. "So? I said I wanted to teach him a lesson. Sure, I took his keys from his pocket. It was easy enough to find the car. He'd parked it on the road just down from Jason's great-aunt's house. I drove the car to a side street near our hotel. I thought he'd come staggering out of the woods, wet and drunk and find the car missing. He shouldn't have been driving in his condition." I wasn't sure her last-minute statement about safe driving had really been her reason for taking Con's beloved car.

"And then next morning you discovered he was dead," I said, trying not to sound judgmental, and that wasn't easy. Yet, she'd looked genuinely heartbroken after his body was discovered.

She nodded. "I was shocked. I didn't think he'd die." I couldn't tell whether she really believed this or whether she'd later wished she hadn't killed the man she loved and who didn't love her back.

"The worst part was knowing I had Con's car. I couldn't leave, it would have looked too obvious. So I waited until my parents were ready to drive home. Then I said I had some people to see in Oxford about the funeral and I'd get a ride back. Once they left, I drove Con's car down here."

"And you thought you got away with it," I said. "Until Jen arrived."

"Her and her nosy questions. She's as bad as you. I knew I couldn't keep Con's car. I was going to get rid of her and the Jensen. There are so many cliffs along the Jurassic Coast. And they're eroding. Park too close to the edge and you could slip over the cliff and down to the sea. Boom."

She looked half-mad, and her eyes glinted when she glanced my way. "I'd have put you in the car with your friend. Getting rid of both of you would have been perfect." Then she scowled. "But just like always, you ruined everything. I hate you more every time I see your smug face."

I wasn't a huge fan of Tina's, either.

She rolled her shoulders as if she was in pain. "And when did you start working out? You never used to be that strong." I felt like telling her I was a witch just to mess with her, but I held my tongue.

"What about the painting?" I asked Tina.

"I don't know if there even was one. Jase and his associates couldn't find it. Jase phoned to ask me if I had it."

"Wait, I thought he closed the punting operation and slipped out of town," I said.

She gave me a superior smirk. "That's what he wanted you to think. He pretended he was one of his own employees and stuck around."

Jen and I stared at each other. I described the young guy who'd charged us a hundred pounds to take out a punt and she agreed that was Con's mate. He'd been so close to us and we hadn't even known it.

So, if the fence didn't have the painting and Tina didn't have it, then once again we were back to the big question.

Where was the portrait of Queen Elizabeth I?

Rafe glanced at me and I gave a small nod. He walked over to the Jensen Interceptor. He paused for just a moment, and I could see that he was bracing himself for more bad news. Then he opened the driver's side door. I watched anxiously. The expression is "my heart was in my mouth," and I'd never felt the truth of that so much. He reached over and opened the glove compartment, and I could tell he'd come up empty. And then, systematically, he began searching the car.

I could tell that Lochlan really wanted to help him, but somehow instinctively we knew this was a task for Rafe and Rafe alone. If he didn't find anything, I was absolutely certain that Lochlan would go over the car again. Pull it to pieces if he had to.

We all watched Rafe's every move. When he reached down under the front seat and pulled out a plastic shopping bag, I allowed myself to hope just a little bit. He opened the bag and looked inside and then rose and came towards me. I couldn't tell from his face whether it was good news or not. And then, in front of all of us, he pulled out the picture of Queen Elizabeth. I know I breathed out a huge sigh of relief.

And Rafe said, looking absolutely stunned, "That vile miscreant put my queen inside a Tesco shopping bag."

I had to bite back a smile. He was as horrified about the indignity as though Connor Townes had taken the actual queen and shoved her in a shopping bag and hidden her inside his car.

I went closer to him and peered over his shoulder. "Is it damaged at all?" I couldn't tell. Queen Elizabeth was looking haughtily back at me, wearing a lace ruff and jeweled head-dress and a gown studded with more jewels. It looked like a perfectly intact painting to me, though any painting that had been hanging for half a millennium was bound to show a little bit of wear.

He was inspecting it minutely. "It appears unharmed."

I couldn't help it. I threw my arms around him. "I am so happy you got her back." Then I turned and threw my arms around Jen. "And I'm so glad I got you back."

I heard a car pull up and assumed it was the police, but to my surprise, Gran, Sylvia, and Alfred came around the side of the garage, presumably to see what was going on. I was quite surprised to see them.

"Gran. What are you doing here?"

She said, "I couldn't get it out of my head that something was wrong. I know you so well, Lucy. I felt that you were putting on your brave voice."

I was tickled. "I have a brave voice?"

"You have indeed. When something dreadful has happened and you don't want me to know, you put on your brave voice. And so I knew we had to come back here and find out what was going on."

Naturally, we filled them in on all the drama. Sylvia went straight to Rafe and peered over his shoulder at the painting. He couldn't seem to stop looking at it.

"Is she unharmed?" Sylvia asked him, as though the painting were the real thing.

He nodded. "I think so. I'll take it to my specialist who cleans my collection, but apart from the indignity of being stored in a common grocer's carrier bag, she's undamaged."

"That is such a relief." And then she turned to Jen. "And are you all right, Jennifer?"

Now that the important piece of property was safe, she could worry about her human friends.

Jennifer said, "Yes. I'm fine. Lucy got here in time."

"Excellent. Well, if we're all fine, I suggest we get back in the car and continue our drive." And then she stopped and looked slightly disappointed. "I suppose we don't need to keep our appointments in St. Ives anymore."

And Rafe, who was as adept at handling Sylvia as anyone I knew, said, "I wish you would. I've got an idea that I want to add something a little more modern to my collection. Now that Lucy's come into my life, I can see how much I've been living in the past. Get them to recommend something modern."

She was delighted with that idea. "I will. And I didn't know what to get you two for a wedding present, so that will be my gift to you. Jennifer can help choose something. I assume she knows your taste?"

She seemed very pleased to have a reason to go nosing through Cornish art galleries.

I said to Jen, "Are you sure you're feeling all right? Maybe we should get a doctor to check you out?"

"I'm fine. I wouldn't trust myself to drive or operate heavy machinery, but I'll sleep on the way to Cornwall." She glanced back. "Do you need me to tell the police what she did to me? I wouldn't want Tina getting away with murder, even if she is your cousin."

Lochlan assured them all that it would be better if they weren't here when the police arrived. I agreed. The fewer vampires or witches on the scene, the better.

Nyx jumped down from Jen's lap and came over to bump my leg. I felt she was trying to tell me something.

As I let myself take in that Jen was absolutely fine and unharmed, I knew I didn't want to lose her again, not even just on a plane back to the States. My crystal ball hadn't led me astray; in fact, it had helped save her life. And that same crystal ball had shown me my best friend in front of the sea.

In my heart, I'd always known it wasn't the coast of the United States. It was Cornwall. I was sure of it.

I said, "Maybe this is terrible timing, but I want you to think about moving here full-time. You could be the manager of the Cornish wool shop." Then I laughed. "It doesn't even have a name. You could help name it, choose the stock. I mean, obviously with my grandmother and Sylvia's help, but they don't want to be running the store day to day, do you?" I said, looking at the two vampires who were following our conversation with interest.

"Certainly not," Sylvia said. "I think you'd be an excellent addition, Jennifer. I hope you'll think about it. We'd be here for any consultation, and of course Agnes will want to work in the shop so you could have time off when you needed it."

I could tell that Jennifer was a little taken aback but also kind of thrilled.

She said, "Really? I've never thought of myself as somebody who worked in retail, but maybe I should give it a try."

I was so excited, I could hardly stand myself. "I think it would be the best thing ever."

She said, "I've never even been to Cornwall. I tell you what, why don't we make this a three-month trial. If it doesn't work, no hard feelings. Our friendship will always come first."

I thought that was an excellent idea. "We'll figure out all the details later, but we have a deal." Nyx made a low sound of approval. She'd obviously figured out the plan long before I did. She was such a smart cat.

Rafe asked Sylvia if she had room for the cat in the Bentley and she graciously said Nyx could come if she didn't sit on Sylvia, herself, which I didn't think was going to be a problem. I was surprised we weren't taking Nyx in the helicopter but I could see how much she'd calmed Jennifer and I'd be catching up with them soon enough.

Jen scooped Nyx up and I followed them out of the garage.

Gran and Sylvia seemed thrilled at the idea of Jennifer as the store manager of our new enterprise, and they were already throwing out ideas for names as they headed to the Bentley. "It should be something to do with fishing, perhaps," Gran suggested. "Like The Fisherman's Net."

"The Fisherman's Knit," Sylvia came back.

"Oh, that's good. That's very good."

"Or something geographical, like Land's End? But for knitters?" They were nearly at the Bentley when Alfred came up with Lamb's End, which had them all cackling as they got into the car.

Jen gave a final wave as she got into the car and I could have sworn Nyx winked at me over her shoulder.

THEY HEADED OFF, and it wasn't long before the police did arrive. By that time, Tina resembled her usual sullen self. Her lips clamped tight, and she refused to speak to anyone. Still, there was Connor's car hidden in her garage, and Lochlan told the attending police officer who he was and that he had suspicions Tina had killed Connor Townes. She was escorted to the station for questioning.

After they'd taken Tina away, I asked, "But will they be able to prove she killed Connor?"

Lochlan said, "Her fingerprints wouldn't have been in the

system. But now, once she's fingerprinted, what do you bet they'll find that one of the many sets of prints they've lifted off that punting pole and the boat will be hers? It's not as good as a confession, but it's very compelling circumstantial evidence."

My poor mom. She was going to hate having a jailbird in the family. Even worse, if she hadn't made me invite my cousin Tina to the wedding, none of this would have happened.

I couldn't wait to tell my mother this. Maybe in the future she'd listen to me when I said I didn't want to do something.

It all seemed a bit anticlimactic now. The police were taking charge of the car and Tina, and Jennifer had continued on with Gran, Sylvia, and Alfred.

I said, "So the murder's solved. The painting's found. It's case closed. Now what?"

Rafe began to chuckle. "Now, my darling, we finally begin our honeymoon." He said, "We'll take the helicopter down to Cornwall, and then Lochlan, you can take it back, and please make sure my Queen is returned to her proper spot in my gallery."

I knew how huge this was that he would entrust the portrait to someone else. But I didn't say anything. We'd delayed our honeymoon long enough. "It would be my pleasure," Lochlan said.

"We'll beat Gran and Sylvia," I said.

"We won't be seeing your grandmother or any more of our friends for at least a week." He sounded so commanding. I raised my eyebrows. "I've booked us into a very private luxury resort on the Scilly Isles. You're going to love it."

I walked up towards him. "Might there be a spa involved?"

"Naturally. Also beautiful beaches, fine dining, everything you could want in a honeymoon."

I didn't want to sound corny, but so long as I had him with me, I already had everything I wanted for my honeymoon. Still, I wouldn't say no to a blissful massage and a pedicure.

Then it occurred to me I didn't have so much as a bathing suit with me. I'd been in such a crazy hurry when I'd thrown a few things in a bag, I didn't even know what was in there. Had I packed a toothbrush? A hairbrush?

As though he'd read my thoughts, he said, "I'll get hold of William and tell him to pack our bags. He can bring them down to us."

"You've thought this through."

"I've been thinking about nothing else for some time."

Lochlan, who'd been watching all of this, said, "Then I think we'd better get started before anything else happens to delay your honeymoon."

Rafe took my hand and laughed. "Excellent plan."

Thanks for reading *Mosaics and Magic*. I hope you'll consider leaving a review, it really helps.

Read on for a sneak peek of Cables and Conjurers, the Vampire Knitting Club Book 15.

Cables and Conjurers, chapter 1

As I walked along the streets of Oxford in the cold March air, my boots rang on the cobblestones. I loved Oxford, and I'd come to think of it as home. I was born in Boston and spent most of my life in the States, but this was always my second home. My grandmother owned a knitting shop here, and she passed it on to me. I didn't work in Cardinal Woolsey's every day; my cousin did that. I was a newlywed, and that kept me pretty busy. It's funny, when I was younger, I used to wonder if I'd marry an older man, but never in my wildest dreams did I think he might be nearly five hundred years older. The truth is, I married a vampire. And, as you might expect, there were some complications, but as my grandmother used to say, even before she was undead herself, you can't fight love. I tried. I think Rafe tried, too. We resisted this feeling we had for each other, but in the end, however long or short our two lives might be, it didn't make any sense to be apart and unhappy. So, I now lived in Crosyer Manor near a small village about half an hour outside of Oxford proper, and I still came in to check on the store.

We'd also opened a second shop in Cornwall, and my best friend, Jennifer, who was American like me and also a witch, ran that. I was super excited because I was going to be seeing Jennifer very soon. She was coming up to Oxford to meet me, and together we were going to take a class on new methods to improve retail sales. I'd been reasonably successful with an online newsletter and shipping various kits and orders around the world, but with two shops, I felt like we could do better. Besides, if I'm honest, I was really excited to get to stay in an actual student dorm room at Saint Benedict's College.

Oxford was all about its colleges. While I'd been inside a few, I'd never stayed overnight, and I was excited to feel like an actual Oxford student. We'd be having breakfast in the Great Hall, which I couldn't even peek inside without thinking of Harry Potter, and then we'd be going to lectures and workshops and later bedding down inside a college that was the better part of a thousand years old. It doesn't get more Oxford than that.

Rafe had laughed at me for insisting I wanted to stay at Saint Benedict's. As he'd pointed out, it was only a half-hour drive back to a very comfortable manor house, but when I explained how much I wanted to have the student experience, he seemed to understand.

Not that I didn't love my opulent, historic, and very comfortable home. It would be easy to settle into just being the lady of the manor. I mean, Crosyer Manor had a butler and everything, and I did like to travel with Rafe whenever possible. He was an expert in antiquarian books and manuscripts and got called all over the world to look at people's collections and authenticate new finds. There was a lot of forgery and fraud in old manuscripts, so having a genuine expert study them was important, and Rafe was the best. Partly because he was around when most of these books were first printed, illustrated, or created, he had a better instinct than most for the authentic. I'd found this retail course online and had been toying with taking it, then Rafe announced he needed to go to Antwerp for a few days, and that settled it. While he was in Antwerp, I would settle into Saint Benedict's College with Jen for three days and study marketing for independent retailers.

"Think of the things I might learn," I'd said to him.

"There are new social media techniques all the time that can help us increase sales."

He looked at me. "Cardinal Woolsey's does quite well as it is. It seems to turn a profit. And you want to be careful not to draw too much attention to the shop, don't forget."

He was referring, of course, to a late-night knitting club that operated in the back room of the knitting shop. Anywhere from eight to twenty vampires showed up frequently in the late evening hours to knit the most incredible creations. I mean, when you've been working at a craft for centuries rather than years, it was amazing how proficient you could get. And they knitted at speeds that not even a machine could rival. However, for obvious reasons, the vampires kept a low profile and were quite happy for Cardinal Woolsey's to remain obscure on the world stage. I had to balance my natural enthusiasm and wish to run a successful business with the need to respect the wishes of these creatures who had not only become my friends but had also helped me solve a few unfortunate murders. The vampires weren't always easy company, but sometimes neither was I. I assured him that I wasn't planning to turn Cardinal Woolsey's into a global franchise; I simply wanted us to do the best we could.

He had to be satisfied with that, and kissing me goodbye, he said, "Just make sure you don't get in trouble."

I was shocked at this advice. "What do you mean? I never get into trouble."

He shook his head at me, and those glacial blue eyes lightened. "Lucy, you never mean to, but trouble seems to find you."

"Well, I don't imagine how trouble could find me when

I'm tucked away in a nice Oxford college learning how to sell a few extra skeins of yarn." I got on my tiptoes and kissed him again. "You make sure you don't get into any trouble in Antwerp."

And with those parting words, I waved him goodbye as he got into his ultra-plush, sleek electric vehicle and carefully backed out, having to avoid Henri the peacock, who was much more a household pet than a wild bird.

I never, ever thought I'd live in a manor house with staff, but I couldn't pretend it wasn't a pleasant experience. William Thresher, Rafe's butler—our butler now, I supposed —was more of a general manager of the property. He loved to cook, and I was the grateful recipient of his talents. He also ran a successful catering business, but his main job was to look after Crosyer Manor and us when we were in residence.

Once Rafe had left for Antwerp, William insisted on making me brunch. "You'll need proper food," he insisted, "to fuel your brain for all the new marketing techniques you'll be learning." He must have known there were plenty of excellent restaurants in Oxford and we had breakfast in the Great Hall as part of our conference package. Still, I didn't argue when he served me eggs Benedict with fresh fruit salad and a cappuccino made exactly the way I liked it from the fancy barista machine in the kitchen. William was devoted to Rafe, but he'd told me more than once how much he enjoyed cooking for someone with a more varied diet.

"Perhaps you'll pass on any good marketing tips to me," he said.

I was in the middle of stabbing a perfect chunk of cantaloupe and glanced up. "But you're turning away work as it is," I reminded him.

"True, I'm very selective, but I like to have enough work to keep Violet busy." Violet Weeks was my cousin, a sister witch, who worked with William on a casual basis, waiting tables while he worked in the kitchen preparing the food.

It became clear to me that William was hovering. I replayed what he'd just said. "Violet also has a day job," I reminded him. She was running Cardinal Woolsey's in my absence. Violet might be family, but she wasn't always the easiest person to get along with. However, she and William seemed to work well together. Better perhaps than she and I did.

William moved a Georgian silver candlestick on the gleaming buffet so it more exactly aligned with the matching candlestick. He wasn't looking at me, but I felt embarrassment coming off him.

I'd always enjoyed William's company, and we got on well. He'd been looking after Rafe for all his adult life, and I felt grateful to him for loyally serving the vampire who'd become my husband. It was unusual for him to act so peculiarly. "Is there something you want to tell me?"

He did turn to me then, finally meeting my gaze. "Would you mind very much if I asked your cousin for a date?" he finally said in a rush.

"Are you sure?" is what came out of my mouth. If I'd thought for a nanosecond, I'd have said something more diplomatic, but he'd taken me by surprise, and I had a habit of blurting out the first thing that came into my head when that happened. Not my finest quality.

William bit back a smile. He wasn't offended, probably because he was used to me. "Frankly, Lucy, I'm not at all sure. But there's something about Violet that I'm drawn to. As you know, I have to be very careful in my personal life. Any woman I shared a future with would need to understand that I can never leave Rafe. And any children I have will take over from me and my sister to serve Rafe."

When Rafe had saved William's many times great-grandfather's life, that earlier William Thresher had made a pledge that his sons would always serve Rafe. So far, that pledge had never been broken. Generation after generation, the oath of loyalty had continued right up to the present day. William ran the house, and his sister was the head gardener for the estate. That kind of loyalty still astonished me.

But what was he saying? "Are you seriously thinking of Violet as your wife and the mother of your children?" I mean, she could be annoying and a know-it-all, but when I left the shop at night, I was free from my irritating cousin. If she married William, she'd be living here. Okay, it wasn't like we'd be crammed into a small apartment together. William had his own quarters, but still. She'd be around.

"It's a long journey from a first date to a marriage," he said in a soothing tone, "but I must marry." He rephrased that. "I want to marry and have children. I'm not sure she's the right person for me, but I'd like to explore the possibility." He'd gone slightly red, I noticed. "With your permission."

"Have you spoken to Rafe about this?" I was trying to buy time so I didn't blurt out something I'd regret.

"No. She's your cousin. I wanted to speak to you first." Now he shifted a pink rose in the already perfect arrangement of fresh flowers on the dining table. "I have no idea if she'd even say yes or if it would go anywhere, but I wanted your permission before I asked her out."

It was the word permission that got me. I understood that

if I said no, he'd forgo any chance of a romance with my cousin. As tempting as it was to nip that relationship in the bud, I couldn't do it. I might not always like Violet, but I wouldn't snatch the possibility of love from her, either. Her dating life had been pretty dismal, and William was a good man. I wouldn't deprive William of romance either. So, putting a firm smile on my face, I said, "William, go for it."

Maybe they'd discover they weren't suited after all. I could only hope.

Having finished my breakfast, I made sure I had my ticket to the conference downloaded to my phone, packed enough clothes for three days at a conference, and prepared to head out. I was going to drive myself, but William insisted on chauffeuring me. "Parking will be terrible," he reminded me. This was true. I'd given Violet the use of my parking spot behind Cardinal Woolsey's as well as the use of the flat above the shop since she ran the place more than I did.

I'd saved Henri a bit of melon, knowing he'd come waddling up to me when I left the house. He had me pegged as a meal ticket, in spite of the fact he was perfectly well fed. He'd been the sorriest excuse for a peacock when I'd first made his acquaintance, with a tail missing a lot of its feathers and a generally bedraggled appearance, but he'd improved a lot. Now that much fuller tail fanned out when I stepped out of the front door, and he danced in a circle. "Oh, you're such a handsome boy," I cooed as he came forward and nipped the treat out of my hand. "Such a handsome boy."

William would have put me in the back seat of the high-end EV Rafe kept for his use, but I refused to act like royalty, and with a sigh he opened the passenger door for me. As we drove, we chatted about his upcoming catering job. With Rafe and me both gone for a few days, he'd taken the opportunity to cook for a movie producer who was renting an estate while filming in Oxford. "You have to tell me if you see any movie stars," I insisted.

"Lucy, they hire me for my discretion as well as my excellent cuisine."

"I'd never tell anyone," I insisted, but he merely sent me a side glance as if to say he didn't want to put me to the test. I'd have argued with him, but since Violet would no doubt do the serving, I could always pump her for info.

He dropped me off in front of the entrance to Saint Benedict's College in the heart of Oxford, and to my delight, Jennifer was walking toward me, dragging a suitcase on wheels. William opened my door for me, and then, as he took my case out of the trunk of the car, I ran forward to give Jen a hug. We squealed, which we pretty much always did when we hadn't seen each other for a few weeks. "It's so great to see you," she said.

"You had your hair cut," I noticed. "It looks great." Jen had probably had about four inches trimmed from her gorgeous, long dark hair, but it was the kind of thing a best friend noticed.

I thanked William, who greeted Jen politely before handing me my own weekender case with wheels, getting back into the car, and pulling out.

"This is so exciting," I said, "staying in a real college." I loved Oxford, as I said, but the truth is, if you didn't go to one of the colleges, you always felt a bit like an outsider. And, being an American, I was already an outsider. Not that a four-day conference was anything like taking a degree, but I thought even having this experience for a few days would give me a peek inside the rarefied world of Oxford and give me a taste of what it would be like to be a student here.

"I can't wait," Jen agreed. "And maybe we'll learn something about marketing."

"If we don't, at least we'll get some catch-up time." We were in touch several times a week as it was, but Cornwall wasn't exactly next door. "How was your trip?" I asked her.

"The train journey was gorgeous. And I walked up from the station."

We walked through the ancient carved arch of Saint Benedict's College and was immediately met by a sign saying "No Admittance." I already felt like an insider since that sign was not for us. We had to go to the porter's lodge, which had been modernized enough that there was a glass door that slid aside for me to walk into the ancient portal and up a couple of stone steps to where modern efficiency met medieval architecture.

A cheerful woman in a flowered dress stood behind a wooden counter and said, "How can I help you?"

"I'm checking in," I said, sounding very proud. Then I explained that I was here for the retail conference, and she looked up my name and passed me a lanyard.

She did the same for Jennifer. We'd requested rooms near each other, and the woman assured us that our rooms were across the hall from each other. Perfect.

As we headed out of the porter's lodge through a different door that led to the main quad, we passed under yet another stone arch. As we did, I felt a cold shiver slide down my neck. It was only a momentary sensation, but I paused and gazed around, feeling as though something, or someone, didn't want me here.

But that was crazy. Jen obviously hadn't felt anything, as she was chatting away. I was letting my imagination run away from me.

~

Order your copy today! Cables and Conjurers, is book 15 in the Vampire Knitting Club series.

To be the first to hear about all of my releases, sign up for my newsletter at NancyWarrenAuthor.com

A Note from Nancy

Dear Reader,

Thank you for reading *Mosaics and Magic*, book 14 in my *Vampire Knitting Club* series. I am so grateful for all the enthusiasm this series has received.

I hope you'll consider leaving a review and please tell your friends who like cozy mysteries.

Review on my website, Amazon, Goodreads or BookBub.

Your support is the wool that helps me knit up these yarns.

If you haven't already, don't forget to join my newsletter for a free prequel, *Tangles and Treason*, the exciting tale of how the gorgeous Rafe Crosyer was turned into a vampire.

I hope to see you in my private Facebook Group. It's a lot of fun. www.facebook.com/groups/NancyWarrenKnitwits

Until next time,
Happy Reading,

Nancy

ALSO BY NANCY WARREN

The best way to keep up with new releases, plus enjoy bonus content and prizes is to join Nancy's newsletter at NancyWarrenAuthor.com or join her in her private FaceBook group Nancy Warren's Knitwits.

❧

Vampire Knitting Club: Paranormal Cozy Mystery

Lucy Swift inherits an Oxford knitting shop and the late-night knitting club of vampires who live downstairs.

Tangles and Treason - A free ebook for newsletter subscribers. A paperback version is available for sale. NancyWarrenAuthor.com

Vampire Knitting Club: Cornwall: Paranormal Cozy Mystery

Boston-bred witch Jennifer Cunningham agrees to run a knitting and yarn shop in a fishing village in Cornwall, England—with characters from the Oxford-set *Vampire Knitting Club* series.

Village Flower Shop: Paranormal Cozy Mystery

In a picture-perfect Cotswold village, flowers, witches, and murder make quite the bouquet for flower shop owner Peony Bellefleur.

Vampire Book Club: Paranormal Women's Fiction Cozy Mystery

Seattle witch Quinn Callahan's midlife crisis is interrupted when she gets sent to Ballydehag, Ireland, to run an unusual bookshop.

Great Witches Baking Show: Paranormal Culinary Cozy Mystery

Poppy Wilkinson, an American with English roots, joins a reality show to win the crown of Britain's Best Baker—and to get inside Broomewode Hall to uncover the secrets of her past.

Abigail Dixon: 1920s Cozy Historical Mystery

In 1920s Paris everything is très chic, except murder.

Murder at the Paris Fashion House - Book 1

Death at Darrington Manor - Book 2

Toni Diamond Mysteries

Toni Diamond is a successful saleswoman for Lady Bianca Cosmetics in this series of humorous cozy mysteries.

Frosted Shadow - Book 1

Ultimate Concealer - Book 2

Midnight Shimmer - Book 3

A Diamond Choker For Christmas - A Holiday Whodunnit

Toni Diamond Mysteries Boxed Set: Books 1-4

The Almost Wives Club: Contemporary Romantic Comedy

An enchanted wedding dress is a matchmaker in this series of romantic comedies where five runaway brides find out who the best men really are.

The Almost Wives Club: Kate - Book 1

Secondhand Bride - Book 2

Bridesmaid for Hire - Book 3

The Wedding Flight - Book 4

If the Dress Fits - Book 5

The Almost Wives Club Boxed Set: Books 1-5

Take a Chance: Contemporary Romance

Meet the Chance family, a cobbled together family of eleven kids who are all grown up and finding their ways in life and love.

Chance Encounter - Prequel

Kiss a Girl in the Rain - Book 1

Iris in Bloom - Book 2

Blueprint for a Kiss - Book 3

Every Rose - Book 4

Love to Go - Book 5

The Sheriff's Sweet Surrender - Book 6

The Daisy Game - Book 7

Take a Chance Boxed Set: Prequel and Books 1-3

For a complete list of books, check out Nancy's website at NancyWarrenAuthor.com

ABOUT THE AUTHOR

Nancy Warren is the USA Today Bestselling author of more than 100 novels. She's originally from Vancouver, Canada, though she tends to wander and has lived in England, Italy, and California at various times. While living in Oxford she dreamed up The Vampire Knitting Club. Favorite moments include being the answer to a crossword puzzle clue in Canada's National Post newspaper, being featured on the front page of the New York Times when her book *Speed Dating* launched Harlequin's NASCAR series, and being nominated three times for Romance Writers of America's RITA award. She has an MA in Creative Writing from Bath Spa University. She's an avid hiker, loves chocolate, and most of all, loves to hear from readers!

The best way to stay in touch is to sign up for Nancy's newsletter at NancyWarrenAuthor.com or www.facebook.com/groups/NancyWarrenKnitwits

To learn more about Nancy and her books
NancyWarrenAuthor.com

Printed in Great Britain
by Amazon

55721716R00141